T0277465

someone

birthed

them

broken

someone

birthed

them

broken

STORIES

ama asantewa diaka

AMISTAD
An Imprint of HarperCollinsPublishers

For all Ghanaian youth—we're the
ones we've been waiting for.

And for all the governments past and
present: the room for improvement
is so vast it looks uninhabited.

This is a work of fiction. Names, characters, places, and incidents are products of the author's imagination or are used fictitiously and are not to be construed as real. Any resemblance to actual events, locales, organizations, or persons, living or dead, is entirely coincidental.

SOMEONE BIRTHED THEM BROKEN. Copyright © 2024 by Ama Asantewa Diaka. All rights reserved. Printed in the United States of America. No part of this book may be used or reproduced in any manner whatsoever without written permission except in the case of brief quotations embodied in critical articles and reviews. For information, address HarperCollins Publishers, 195 Broadway, New York, NY 10007.

HarperCollins books may be purchased for educational, business, or sales promotional use. For information, please email the Special Markets Department at SPsales@harpercollins.com.

FIRST EDITION

Designed by Kyle O'Brien
Art © Ama Asantewa Diaka
Photo on page 9 © Ssorensen/Shutterstock

Library of Congress Cataloging-in-Publication Data has been applied for.

ISBN 978-0-06-325955-3

24 25 26 27 28 LBC 5 4 3 2 1

list of characters in
someone birthed them broken

key:

——— = dating
═══ = friends
------- = exes

——→ = parent to child
←——→ = siblings

god or whatever

KUSI OPOKU AGYEMANG SNR.

I have seen Mamaa mistake a slow-healing wound for a God who listens. She and Nnena were in the backseat of an old Golf when Nnena's nephew drove through an amber light, skidded dangerously off the street in an attempt to prevent a head-on collision with a dirty white Beetle, and crashed into a roasted corn stall, whose owner had thankfully crossed the road to deliver soft but slightly burnt corn to a customer. It would've been an excellent save, if the impact of the crash hadn't forced the hex bolts securing the front seats to loosen, causing them to collapse on the frail legs of two old ladies. It took Mamaa eight and a half weeks for her wounds to fully heal and to walk without a painful limp, and she swore it was the God in her, never mind that God rarely answered her prayers correctly. Never mind that this God of hers silently watched her cry out as her only son was dying (and if you've heard an anguished woman's cry, you know its potential to impale an eardrum). Never mind that this same God knew of the arthritis that had been trudging in her bones for over a year, and did nothing about it. But I guess when all you have is rheumatoid arthritis and faith in God, believing becomes an easy act.

Personally, God is great and all, I'm glad he exists to occupy so much of Mamaa's time so I can have this old house to myself on Sunday mornings and Wednesday evenings without her incessant complaints bouncing off its pink walls, but there was simply no time for him in my schedule. Between struggling to take care of my five-and-a-half-year-old daughter, whose mother dropped her off for a weekend a year ago and never returned, making sure there's enough money for the upkeep of all eight of my younger siblings, a heavily pregnant girlfriend who used to love my presence and my penis, and trying to keep Mamaa from complaining, I didn't have time for a God who decided to show up when and how he wanted.

Mamaa has always been more of a mother than a grand-mother to me. She gave birth to my father when she was only seventeen, and my father had me when he was just a year away from turning twenty. So when I was born Mamaa was still a young and beautiful woman. A mother who had a list of disappointments taller than her five-foot-four self, so in order to occupy her loss of faith in men, she poured all her affection into her son. And the problem with making your son the only man in your life is that your love becomes oversized, it covers too much skin, it doesn't draw his personhood out well, and it hides his true form from you. Perhaps, if my father had borne the responsibility of raising me, he wouldn't have had kids like a child squirting pee.

Having to maintain the family's cocoa farm since my father passed away is aging me. I'm only thirty-nine, I should be dating three girls from different neighborhoods and plotting 101 ways of not getting caught. I should be taking long drives with a busty girl the boys in the town call "wild and carefree" because she likes giving blow jobs from the front seat of spacious cars, and shrugging off rumors of littering the whole of Mampong with broken hearts. Instead I spend my dawns calculating the difference between sales made and salaries to be paid. This morning when I saw my reflection in the mirror, my skin looked like someone had run a marathon in rubber boots on it. You would think with all the work I'm being forced to do, I would gain some muscles, yet here I am—two steps away from looking like a bag of bones. The price of everything has gone up: transport costs are ridiculously high, the price of food has increased twice already this month and July hasn't even ended! I used to buy one small bucket of fish with 1,000 cedis for Alice to cook three different stews, but now that can barely pay for a small bowl of fresh redfish. My father should come and see what has become of Ghana; even to his dying day he was so far up the ass of nostalgia that he believed all Ghana needed was another Nkrumah to thrive. Now we have an Nkrumahist for a president, but with all of Hilla Limann's bravado and intellect, what has he been able to do for the cocoa industry? It's 1981 already; yes, he's ended the shortage of food and basic social amenities, but an industry that carried the entire weight of the country is still failing. I can't even pay the wages of all the farmhands, much less save some to finish building a new kitchen for Mamaa.

I have forgiven my father for a lot of things. I have forgiven him for leaving his older children to parent his younger children. I have forgiven the unhinged women he often brought home, especially the one who left a boomerang-shaped scar above my left eyebrow. I have forgiven him for making me carry the weight of a firstborn son when I should have been enjoying the benefit of a middle child. I have even forgiven him the stupidity of fathering nine children, when he never wanted to have even one in the first place, but I absolutely cannot forgive him for dying.

Sometimes I wonder if he would have lived a different life if he knew he was going to die before his fifty-fourth birthday. I wonder, even, how different he would've been if he had been sick for a longer time. The first stroke didn't harm him much; in fact, he didn't even realize it was a stroke, he just mentioned to Mamaa that in the afternoon a sudden wave of dizziness overcame him, he couldn't see very well, and although he wanted to call out to someone, he couldn't make enough sense of words to even form them. But the feeling went away after ten minutes, so Mamaa prayed for him and put him to bed after making him soup, planning to take him along to her next hospital visit, which was scheduled in two weeks. But eleven days later he had another stroke, and within hours he was dead. Just like that. A ruptured vessel bled into his brain, they said. I wonder if he would have been more patient, more accommodating of his children's needs, more interested in our lives if he had been sick longer. Maybe even gotten around to believing in the God his mother swore by instead of placating his disbelief by paying her tithe money to a God he didn't really care for.

I found it funny. You know? His death. Not the throw-your-head-back-and-laugh kind of funny. Just funny in the way you spend weeks tilling the soil, planting and preparing for the rains in July, only for the clouds to decide not to open up. I imagined my father old and wrinkled with bad knees, his lean body slowly giving way for fat to settle in his belly. I imagined him frustrated with his sons for repeating his mistakes and burdened by the men his daughters brought home. Hell, I even imagined him begging for the company of his grandchildren to soften the brunt of loneliness that came with aging. Instead, on the fifth anniversary of his death we all wore white and had goat light soup with cold beer like it had been perfectly okay for him to die.

Mamaa resents me. But it wasn't always like this. In the blessed days of my childhood, she was something of a doting grandmother. Before her grandchildren turned her from a mother to a matriarch. Before supermarkets became a thing in the streets of Osu and before they fixed the road connecting Accra to Aburi. Before her bones creaked and her face creased. Before she outlived her only son. One of those women who lent their backs to be used as tables for their grandchildren's homework when their own sons had crouched on hard floors to learn how to write. I remember the melody that sprang from her throat when she found out I'd passed my sixth-form exams, the bend in her voice as she broke into song, infected by joy, life stretching into her words as she hugged my body into mush. I remember when my first child was born, when the fear of my daughter's sheer existence had lurched me into lethargy. How quickly she took over planning the naming ceremony, cooking food to feed more than fifty people, transforming the front yard into a space decent enough to hold the ceremony, with enough drinks for everyone and even the akpeteshie that the baby had to taste to initiate her into the world, pulling yards of patterned white lace no one knew existed from her room to clothe the family, the burst of pride when she found out I was naming the child after her—Oye. Maame Oye; a good thing. I knew then how much she loved me, and I know now how deeply she resents me. I even know the exact time the rot began, how it neatly coincided with the realization that her God was not going to bring her son back to life. I know it well, but I don't really mind, or allow myself to care too much about it. It is incidental resentment—old comfortable woman who has spent all her youth on her only son and his children is waiting patiently for him to build her a house so she can die peacefully, loses said son to a sudden illness and is left with grandchildren and great-grandchildren, who not only drain her of the little cash and strength she has, but can't even sustain the family cocoa farm well enough to build her a small kitchen. I've been living with her resentment since my father died. I would be worried if it stopped.

It is Alice Aba Bentsifi who is the root of my migraines. Dark-skinned women with slits for eyes, and soft bums that sink in when you drill a hole with your finger, will be the death of me. Honestly. Because that woman has a mouth just like Mamaa, and you would think I would run in the opposite direction. But look at me—all desire, no brain. I haven't gathered the courage to tell Mamaa yet that I have a son on the way. She already looks at me as though recklessness and womanizing have been passed down genetically.

I want to stop loving women. I want to stop thirsting for a mouthful of satisfaction at the front door of Alice's skin. I want to stop needing her acceptance of me. I want to stop feeling a sense of doom when she distances herself from me. This love thing is a myth because here I am, adjudged the title of a devil and a young woman's nightmare. Relationships are self-destructive tendencies, I tell you. And I clearly will never understand women. Why will you go ahead and keep a baby when I have made it very evident from the onset of this relationship that I do not want any more kids? All I want to do is love this woman, love her down to the skin of an orange cleaned out of all its juice, seed, and fiber. But instead she's allowing a child to foster rage in her bosom. I wanted nothing to do with children. I wanted a carefree love, not the kind of carefreeness that lends itself to recklessness, but the kind that had a laser focus on joy. A fun love, full of laughter and good sex. Nothing like my father's. I wanted nothing to do with continuing his maddening legacy of birthing children he didn't want. I only wanted to cruise through the act of lovemaking, a little less tense and a lot more loved.

But now I have become a devil of a man for not wanting another child. Both love and God are myths, because Alice swears she loves me, and Mamaa swears I'm lucky God loves me even though I don't acknowledge him. Yet they both fail me. Frauds.

Alice swears she never wants to see me again, but she still sends word through her cousin for me to name the child. I don't understand women. I wish I could just take a holiday and forget about her, but the boy looks like I squeezed him out of my scrotum, there's no way he's not mine.

The walls lean in, each corner caving in as the paint peels off. I know this feeling well, this stifling responsibility.

He's a Wednesday-born. Just like his father.

Kweku. Nana Kweku Opoku Agyemang. She should name him that. And for his own sake, I hope God shows up in his life, because I'm too busy getting mine together.

Graphic Daily

50p THUR, FEB 5, 1981. No 9432

Imoru Egala fights on for restoration of eligibility

Alhaji Imoru Egala is mostly known for his role as a former foreign minister; what many aren't privy to is his pivotal role and vision as the founder of the People's National Party. It may well be seen as a sign of rebellion—after being barred by a commission set up by the military government in 1966, preventing him from running as PNP candidate in the 1979 general and presidential elections, he nevertheless sponsored the candidacy of Mr. Limann. Last January, Mr. Egala began a court action against the electoral commissioner seeking a court ruling restoring his eligibility for public office. Twelve months later, he still fights on.

Ghana's sickening mortality rate

Last year, the total number of infants who didn't make it past twelve months was 731 in total. Maternal mortality remains a challenge in providing quality maternal and other reproductive health-care services in Ghana. Lack of logistics, medical and laboratory equipment, inadequate knowledge about the benefits of antenatal care services as well as non-adherence of healthcare workers to treatment protocols and standard operating procedures were found as major setbacks to the provision of effective and quality maternal healthcare services in Ghana. It is, therefore, imperative for the government of Ghana and other non-governmental organizations to invest in strengthening the health-care delivery system, especially in rural Ghana, by making available basic logistics, medical and laboratory equipment, as well as improving upon maternal health education, and consistently organizing capacity building training programs for healthcare workers.

MORE HANDS NEEDED

. . . on cocoa farms in the south

In a bid to return to the glory days of Ghana being the world's largest cocoa producer, the government of Ghana is keen on expanding production of cocoa. In the 1960s, Ghana was producing an average of 450,000 tons per year. Now we can't even manage half that. We're producing as low as 159,000 tons a year! Farmers all over the country complained bitterly of the black pod—a disease that causes widespread destruction of cocoa—and the high prices of treatment needed to prevent it from spreading.

The government of Ghana is providing seedlings to over three hundred farmers in the Ashanti region alone; Volta, Eastern, and Central region farmers are set to receive their share in the coming months.

However, these farmers will need an inflow of laborers to handle the labor-intensive work to be done.

NOT A REAL NEWSPAPER

the year i turned twenty-three

BOATEMAA

An exaggerated puff. That's what my mother described me as when she was speaking with her friend over the phone. She drew a large mound of breast on her chest as she spoke, as though the person on the phone could see her gesturing. The minute I hit puberty my mother started dressing me like she was storing hot food in between layers and layers of leaves, as if she was trying to hide my body from the world. The kids in my school called me Breastina Naa Forfor Forson and Miss Lolo. Some of them even called me surplus, because according to them it wasn't so much that big breasts were suddenly a weird phenomenon, it was that the rest of my body did not correlate with my chest. What even were 34F boobs doing in a size 0 body? Once, because he couldn't remember my name, Mr. Osei, the social studies teacher, called me Breasticles. But exaggerated puff? That was new. It was said in a tone of wonder, like she couldn't believe I was her daughter. Couldn't believe a body like mine came out of a body like hers. She had told me before that if we didn't share the same gnarly map of a birthmark on our wrists, she could've sworn I wasn't hers. My mother came from a line of petite women with small breasts and bodies chock-full of anxiety. Was it the time she saw the love letter Kojo Gaisie wrote for me on Vals Day? The one that had "Your breasts are like two fawns, like twin fawns of a gazelle" in it, and he swore my breasts had turned him into a poet like he didn't lift that phrase word for word from a Song of Songs verse. No matter what I told my mother, she was convinced I was in school lifting my blouse for boys to see. Or is it anytime she calls me more than three times and I don't call back within an hour? Anxiety was good neighbors with my mother and nobody could easily tear them apart. Not even my father, a soft sac of a man who had yielded so much to my mother's insecurities they had morphed into his original thoughts. He only protested her excesses over his autonomy, but when she projected her anxieties on me, suddenly, her word was bond. Anxiety racked my mother's body well; it started as pain pummeling her chest, and manifested visibly as a running stomach. At least twice every month, something I would do or say, or not do or say, would give my mother anxiety. I wasn't sure if it was her anxiety or if it was that my body had an etched "need to be overprotected" sign on my fore-head, but my mother was very very overprotective. As a child I was rarely out of her sight, closer than her handbag. The only reason I spent all my primary education at Albright Academy was because it was a ten-minute walk from our house in Kasoa and it gave my mother comfort that she could pass by anytime to check on me. I didn't go to boarding school because the thought of her not seeing me for days and days on end was unbearable to her. And so when it was time for me to begin my first year at Methodist University College, even she could tell that the fifty-seven-minute commute was ridiculous, so she got me a one-bedroom apartment that was a few minutes away from campus. Took an extra key for herself and sent me off half-heartedly. It was a very difficult decision for her. How could it not have been? I was the only child she bore for my father—a man whose family had openly disliked her—after two years of marriage. Which meant I was a source of both pride and fear. But I was filled with joy. I was twenty and desperate to carve out an identity for myself beyond being my mother's daughter. Desperate to live my own life so I had real stories to write in English papers about how my holiday went instead of recounting staying indoors with my mother. I wanted a life outside of my bedroom, outside of our house and the twelve flower pots in the front yard. I wanted the life the girls in my high school talked about. The boys and the accompanying heartbreak, the clothes, the adventures, and the nights out. I wanted a life that I, Boatemaa, could call my own.

The first two years of university were great. Dzidzor, who was majoring in marketing, lived in the apartment above me. Our individual schedules didn't allow us to see each other often but we were always texting. Slowly, brick by brick, I began to build boundaries for the relationship I had with my mother. I waited an hour before returning her calls, then two, then four. Limited her visits to once a week instead of twice a week. And even though my very first relationship had ended (after six and a half months because he had to leave the country and, according to him, he "couldn't do long distance"), when my mother asked me about boys, I told her I was talking to a boy I really liked.

When I was twenty-two I met a man with skin so dark you could capture a shot of it for a color spectrum and hair so soft it was almost sinful to touch. Within ten seconds of meeting him, he scratched his balls and stuck out the same hand to shake mine with. I hoped the bewildered look I wore would shrink his hand back to his side, but he looked up at my face, looked at his hand, and turned to me. "Don't worry, my balls are clean." It was the ridiculousness of his entirety, from his ashy knees to his six-foot-seven frame, too-tight shorts, dusty old shoes as if he had been trekking for miles, and boyish grin jumping out of a man's face, to his my-balls-are-clean-so-you-can-shake-my-hand, that tickled the giggle out of me. A few months later, I was sitting on his linoleum bedroom floor, wearing cute black cotton panties I had bought in traffic, and switching channels like I paid half of his rent.

I didn't tell him this but Opoku was the first man I called beautiful; if he were a comic character he would be the type whose features were in symmetry. Hair like a neatly trimmed hedge. Not-too-big, not-too-small head, sitting on top of pointed shoulders, his every movement as graceful as a dancer's. He was also the first man to not obsess over my breasts. To not treat them like the highlight reel of a new movie. To not hinge my beauty and his desire solely on my breasts like other men did. Instead, he pored over every stretch of skin on my body, drew out the ordinary like it was something special. He thought I had the perfect set of shiny, evenly arranged teeth. He found the dark shade of my upper lip artistic, nibbled on my upper arm because the softness of it somehow made him feel safe, and made my stomach his resting place. He was easy to love because he saw me fully, clearer than even I did. I spent all of Tuesdays and Thursdays in his T-shirts at his place because there were no lectures. I spent the days watching movies he had downloaded for me, picking out onions from food we bought from the junction before eating because he hated seeing them, and watching him sketch in big drawing pads. He was currently obsessed with photos of James Barnor. He had printed a bunch of them from the internet and spent several hours drawing near-perfect pencil sketch versions of his photos. He was planning to hold an exhibition of them once he was done. My favorite so far was the one of the woman in the green dress holding green and red plastic gallons. Mostly because she reminded me of my mother. Opoku was going to be more famous than James Barnor one day. At least that's what he told me, and I believed him. I know how this looks—you're probably thinking, *Can we say a little prayer for our sister who left the bulk of her brains on a fluffy pillow on the way to love?*—but he used sixty-three minutes to sketch me in perfect line detail; that's a good enough reason to anchor your faith in anybody's half-formed talent. Some people are great at learning any craft and some people are naturally good at things, and Opoku was comfortably nestled in the latter. He could draw anything, I'm serious—anything! So even though I initially thought it was pretty naïve and a little stupid of him (just a little) to quit his job as a graphic designer in a small printing firm to follow his Basquiat dreams, in the hopes that he would one day become a reference point in secondary school textbooks like James Barnor, something about his intense penetrating stare coordinating with his large hands convinced me. Besides, he wasn't saddled with the burden of paying rent (thanks to an inherited family house) and was steadily eating through his share of money from the two-year advance rent his uncle had collected from the tenant living in his late father's house. He spent his days wearing the same faded jean shorts with no boxers, sketching everything and anything, tweeting his artwork and retweeting all his compliments, telling anyone who would listen to join Twitter because Facebook was so 2000 and late, as if we were a hundred years into the 2000s and it wasn't a dry March in 2012. He was only thirty; when best to be young and free if not now? I believed in him. He was going to be great. #youngandgifted.

One Monday afternoon we drove from Awudome roundabout—with its half-weed, half-grave cemetery, half-baked roads, and old buildings—to East Legon's shiny new roads and monochrome-painted buildings, so I could audition for a role in an Indomie instant noodles ad. I had told him about looking for something that would bring me extra income outside of the pocket money my parents gave me. Something that worked with my timetable and paid well. Someone in my class was making extra cash writing essays for people, but that was too much work for me; I wanted something easy and good. I wasn't much of an actor—I wasn't an actor at all—but he had spoken about me to one of the agents, an old friend of his, like I brought out little pellets of gold after every shit, so I went ahead anyway. Plus if I got picked for the ad, I would earn a hefty amount. We climbed up a narrow staircase to a red door, where he rubbed my back and wished me good luck.

The smell of coffee was the first thing that greeted me when I stepped in. A woman in an oversized yellow shirt smiled at me, told me her name was Cynthia, asked me what my name was with a slight lisp (which I found sexy), and handed over a sheet with five short sentences for me to read out loud.

"Brilliant. Read it again, but this time, with more attitude," she said, still smiling.

I had to pretend a taste of heaven had been evenly distributed on my taste buds and smile a little too aggressively, gesturing wildly. After six takes, I was ready for it to end. My cheeks were beginning to hurt. With a rehearsed smile, she told me I would hear back from them. I smiled back and told her I would expect her call, but we both knew that was our last smile.

There are different ways to notice that you have fallen in love with someone. Rose from my business class fell for Adams because he unashamedly pronounced *issue* as "eye-sue." Abie in my programming class said the day Kuuku gave her a lap dance was the day she knew she had found "The One." And Pinamang swore she would marry Carl because he felt no shame farting around her on their first date. On the drive back from the audition, we passed over a pothole that shook my whole body. My breasts wobbled underneath my dress. Opoku looked over at me and apologized for the bad road like it was his fault the country had shitty roads. That was the moment I fell for him.

There's something about brokenness that makes you want to pass your fingers on cracked surfaces and trail them on their sharp edges, you know? Just to be able to tell how truly broken they are. Opoku was the poster child for a lost boy living in a man's body. His refusal to forgive a father who was absent left me unsettled. Some days his rage felt magnified, but what did I know? I had a very present father whose only sin was staying in the shadow of my mother. I had never heard anyone speaking of their father with such disdain. The way he talked about his father could freeze falling rain. A low-life-cheating-three-timing-good-for-everything-but-being-a-father who quickly discarded his mother the minute she was pregnant, as though his arrival was an impending doom. He held on tightly to his anger. It was like a stain he wasn't even interested in getting out. He wore it loudly. His brokenness called out to me; it yelled my name out loud in silence and begged for salvation.

He would occasionally run out of money and commit to eating one heavy meal a day. Although he insisted it wasn't a big deal, I worried too much about him starving and ended up cooking for him, or ordering food to be delivered to him.

After he complained bitterly about losing his audience and having to start from scratch because his Twitter account had been suspended, I created a mailing list for him and got ninety-eight people to sign up. He sent one newsletter and abandoned it. One time he went into a fit of rage because an obituary poster of a sixty-eight-year-old man reminded him of his father. And when I suggested therapy he looked at me as if I knew nothing of the world. I carried a cross of salvation for someone who didn't want saving.

The sex was sticky, too sweet, lacking in shame and abundant in touch. The way our bodies fit into each other. It was like discovering there was more than one way to enjoy a mango: you didn't have to only make a small hole through the skin of the fruit to suck out the juice, you could gently peel off the skin and sink your teeth into its sweetness. A never-ending want for skin and teeth and the harmonic movement of bodies.

One Friday he came over to my end because the construction noise was too loud for him to get any work done. His uncle was building an outhouse in their house to accommodate a second tenant. We lay naked in my bed, bodies juxtaposed on each other, the damp soles of our feet staining an already stained wall. Besides the shadowy outline of our naked forms on sky-blue sheets, the room's stillness was absolute. An unexpected knock on the front door jolted my knee. I had locked the door and left the key sticking in as he pulled my panties off earlier. I could hear my mother's voice calling out impatiently for me to open the door. She had an extra key, but with my key in the lock she couldn't get in. Gripped with fear, I suddenly couldn't find a piece of clothing. It must have taken just about a minute to find a dress and pull it over my head but it felt like hours in the frenzy. Opoku, slightly terrified and trying hard not to show it, slipped into his clothes, rushed to the living room, and stretched his long body on the sofa, assuming a position as though he were fast asleep. I don't know what it is about the fear of being caught that makes one act even more stupid. The minute my mother walked in, she knew. She could smell it in the air even before she looked at me. The disappointment in her eyes was to be expected; it was the painful sigh that tipped me slightly off-balance. It was pointless telling her he'd just come over to take a nap.

"Abrantie, wo firi he?"

My mother's voice shook with anger as she drilled him. Asking him where he was from, who his mother was, what his father did, what church he attended, what intentions he had for her daughter. As though she was about to marry me off and was mentally making notes to make sure I wasn't tied to the devil. It was the longest fifteen minutes of my life. I wanted to become one with the sofa. Months after, Opoku and I would laugh about it, and create alternative scenarios, some where he hid under the bed to avoid my mother altogether, some where he told my mother the truth about his wavering belief in one true God and his blatant animosity towards Christianity—hence his no-church rule—instead of telling her he was a staunch member of the Methodist Church.

After he left, my mother didn't pick up my calls or speak to me for seven long days. And when she finally did, she dished out monosyllables as if there were a shortage of words in her belly. I wasn't sure what I was being punished for—that I had a man in my life or that I was having sexual relations. Mothers hold grudges like abandoned lovers too. But it eventually eases out and transforms into blowing up your phone every single minute they can spare in an attempt to track your every move, disguised as overprotective love.

When I was seventeen, I laughed at my classmate Worla till I peed on myself because she thought BJ stood for "bare jokes." I didn't think it was possible for one person to be this monstrously naïve. So I was a bit thrown off when I became the one to be laughed at the year I turned twenty-three.

It was a quarter past six in the evening when I got Dzidzor's text. I remember because the lights had been off for twenty-four hours and the kids in the neighborhood broke into a chorus of "light aba oooo light aba!" the minute electricity was restored.

"Which contraceptive is the best to use to avoid pregnancy right after sex?"

"Um, I dunno," I texted back.

"Really? You guys use condoms all the time?"

"Um . . . no, we don't. We used to, but not anymore."

"If you don't use condoms then what contraceptives do you use?"

"We don't use condoms, his pull-out game is strong. Opoku says condoms are for niggas who don't know how to control their dicks lol."

"OMG! HAHAHAHAHAHAHAHAHAHA, Boatemaa! Pull-out game strong? Oh my god! Condoms are for everybody with a dick who doesn't want a child or an STD. Girl what? If you don't get a contraceptive that works for you. You kill me LMAO."

Shame turned my giggle into an awkward laugh. I should've known this, and deep down, a part of me knew it was careless of us. We had been using condoms the first two months of our relationship, but Opoku hated it and swore he would be careful, and so far, he really had been. We'd been dating for almost eight months now and I was yet to have a pregnancy scare. Dzidzor didn't forget or forgive my ignorance. It came up in every conservation; she laughed at me for an entire year until it finally became a thing too stale to poke at.

In late April we are fighting too much. We've been a couple for eleven months but it feels like several lifetimes. He calls less and less, and when we're together he's not as present as I know him to be: he stops resting his head on my stomach, rarely sketches in my presence, flirts too much, borrows money from me that he never returns, gets me nothing for my twenty-third birthday and swears he will make it up to me. Introduces me to an art collector we met at an event as a "good friend" because "I just met her, no need to tell her about my personal life," as if my identity as his girlfriend reduced his chances of being an artist. He kisses a black girl with a South London accent right in front of me while getting his car washed in the neighborhood car park, and tells me the mere fact that he did it right in front of me should tell me it means nothing. The first reaction to pain is always disbelief. Not anger, not hurt, but disbelief.

Disbelief that one plus one could possibly equal zero. Disbelief that people can be unapologetically disappointing. And then, slowly, it shape-shifts into anger. The kind of anger that festers like an open wound, needing just one more touch to transition into fatality.

I notice the familiarity of another girl's name on his lips. He tells me it is a name he has given to his imaginary friend, a make-believe friend whose presence he escapes into to release all burdens. He tells me it's the same thing I do with keeping journals, an alternative to the therapy session I've been blabbing about. I wonder briefly what I would call an imaginary friend if I had one. The fighting doesn't stop much. I know I should leave. I threaten to leave. He swears he needs me. I beg to be loved well—just like in the beginning of us, like he first loved me. He tells me he loves me still, but everything he says and does deepens the wound of heartbreak. I know I don't belong here. But somebody etched hope into my palms and tricked me into believing it would save our relationship. I had gone and subjected my heart to a belief system where giving resulted in getting. And so I stay.

I stay silent despite the ache of wanting to talk things out, the false belief that talking things out—listening and being heard—will fix us, the want for simplicity, for newness and going back to the feeling of being apologized to because of potholes. I'm miserable and I want to call my mother and have her figure out everything from just the weak hello I will offer. But my ache for independence had erected a boundary between us, and she had learned how to tiptoe around me. It doesn't get any more adulthood than twenty-three, so I ignore the want. My third year of uni is almost over; in spite of myself, I make good grades for the first semester. I'm happy with my progress but at the same time anxious for my final year. Anxious about the work I have to do to complete, anxious about the future, what happens when my time in school is over. Do I let go of this tiny apartment with its old louvre blades, beige white walls, and cold floors? Will Opoku and I be okay?

I am nauseated all the time. Everything tastes like betrayal. We have a big fight over yet another girl he claims is nobody. He hasn't called in ten days. I want to say that I'm a strong independent woman who respects people's space and that's why I haven't called him, but every time I open my messages and see him online, I die a little inside.

I run to the bathroom to throw up. I am certain it's not my period. I had it less than three weeks ago; although it had been lighter than usual, it hasn't been twenty-nine days yet. Plus he pulled out so it's fine. He always pulls out. My body is just grieving his nonchalance. I haven't been eating well, a combination of poor diet and a broken heart, so my body can't even keep to schedule. Besides, I was taking antibiotics for an ear infection. Everything was just making it so hard for my body to keep up.

Three weeks later and it's not fine. It's 2:16 a.m. and I'm awake and in pain. I figure I'm about to get my period, hence the pain, so I just suck it in and attempt to fall back asleep. But the pain gets worse by the hour. It's 5 a.m. now and the pain is so bad I can barely walk from my room to the bathroom.

I lie still and take deep breaths, naming each inhalation after a letter of the alphabet, hoping I fall asleep before I hit Z. On P, I feel a gushing sensation. I crawl to the bathroom, pull my pants down, and that's when I see the blood. I call Dzidzor in a fit of tears; she shows up in less than five minutes and takes me to the hospital.

I'm not sure if it's a mixture of disinfected floors, a swarm of sick people, and the intermittent pain invading my body that's making me dizzy and nauseated. Dzidzor is convinced food will make me a lot more stable, so she leaves to go buy hausa koko. A nurse with a friendly smile calls me in a few minutes after she's left. A homely looking doctor with a toothy grin and a deep resounding voice does a pelvic exam and an ultrasound. He rubs my back gently and tells me I'm having a miscarriage.

I look back at him with a mixture of shock and terror.

"How?" I blurt out.

"Fifteen percent of pregnancies end in miscarr—"

"How am I miscarrying? I haven't missed my period in two months. How?"

He looks back at me.

The word is rolling itself in my head. Over and over. *Miscarriage.*

He rubs my back again and asks a series of questions. I can't get the word out of my head. After what seems like forever he tells me I can wait for nature to do its thing or I can have a surgical procedure. I feel my phone vibrate in my pocket. I want it to be him, but it's just Dzidzor telling me she's at the waiting area with hot hausa koko. I want to ask her what to do but I remember how hard she laughed at me the last time we talked about condoms, and I swallow my tears. I want the world to stop spinning for a few minutes so I can make sense of everything but I'm too confused to form sentences in my head. So instead, I tell her the doctor wants to keep me for a couple of hours, and could she please come back after noon.

I opt for a surgical procedure because it sounds like the easier way out.

In the operating room, I lie flat on the table, eyes firmly fixed on the ceiling. I juggle pity and anger and fear. Self-pity at the thought of being here all by myself. I never imagined this would happen and that it would happen this way. Upset with Opoku for us fighting and, by virtue of it, his not being here. In spite of the doctor's comforting words, I'm terrified of having to do this procedure. Will I be in pain? What happens after? Will it affect me in the future? The doctor squeezes my hand gently and mumbles something. I'm sure the anesthesia is working because I can feel myself fade away. Everything goes black.

Dzidzor comes back right when the pharmacist has handed over my required drugs. The minute we sit in the taxi I tell her everything. She's too stunned to speak, and for once, I'm grateful for the silence. We spend the rest of the ride with her cradling my hands and apologizing over and over again as if she caused my pain. Back home I crawl into bed and finally allow myself to cry. I try to think my way through the pain, but nothing prepares me for how much it hurts, how it aches so much when I didn't even know which decision I would make if I had known I was pregnant. I'm not sure I'm allowed to grieve.

But I do. The idea that a fetus had begun to take form in my body plagues my thoughts. When precisely did it happen? Was it the Monday we had make-up sex after two hours of screaming at each other? Or was it the evening after my B. Comms. mid-test? I had been too stunned to ask the doctor questions, but Dzidzor said her sister had miscarried because she took antibiotics. I took antibiotics too; was that what caused it? What would Opoku have done? What will he do now?

Five days pass by quietly. I'm too weak to make it to class, and too nauseated to keep food down. I feel a sadness so vast it muffles my voice. I feel the vibration of my ringing phone somewhere on the bed. It's my mother calling.

"Temaa, enti sɛ manfrɛ wo a, wonfrɛ me bi?"

"Hello, Mummy, I was actually going to call you this evening," I lie.

"What's wrong? Is everything okay? You don't sound good."

"I'm okay, I just have a bit of a headache so I'm lying in bed." Which wasn't a complete lie.

"Should I come over?" I imagined her squinting, something she always does when she is worried, as if she suddenly needed to see better to comprehend her feelings.

"No, Mummy, I'm fine, really. I've taken a painkiller and I just had something to eat. I'm sure I'll be fine by morning."

She sighs heavily into the phone, and it sounds like a soft breeze.

"All right, I'll call you in the evening." I feel the threat of a sob swelling in my throat. To think a few months ago she would've been standing outside of my door unannounced, and yet here she was giving room to my privacy. I feel a sudden urge to tell her everything.

"Mummy . . ." I am weighed down by fear and the urge to tell her leaves as quickly as it came.

"Boatemaa?"

"I miss your abenkwan. I can't remember the last time I had some with fufu."

"When you come home, I'll make some for you. Okay?" I can hear the smile in her voice.

Two weeks pass without hearing from Opoku. My anger is a plot of land that by now has a foundation and a first floor. He should be the one calling and texting me. He should be the one apologizing. He is the one who had a girl sending naked pictures of herself in his DMs. Telling me he had no control over what other people wanted to send to him online and accusing me of overreacting over someone he hadn't even had any intimate relations with was bullshit. But I'm tired of fighting so I send him a text message. It's short and has only one sentence. "I'm still angry with you."

I feel entitled to a response for being the first person to reach out. I'm not prepared for the silence that follows. It infuriates and confuses me, and I'm convinced he needs to see me for the silence to end. But there's more of it when I show up at his door. Suddenly I can no longer contain my anger. I fling a plastic gift bag across his face so swiftly it cuts him right above his left eye.

The guilt that immediately followed took a long time to

leave my body. He wore his wounded eye like a badge; posted it three times on social media with a different caption for each picture and ended his sentences with "LOL" like it was a joke he expected everyone to get. I spent months wondering if the folly I committed in my moment of anger nullified my pain.

I'm twenty-six, it's 2016, and I still weigh 59 kilograms and in my head I am taller than five feet eight. I'm sitting beside the window in a small blue bus, with my face pressed against the dirty windowpane, allowing the air to baptize my face. There are two teenage girls sitting beside me. It's hard not to eavesdrop. One is telling the other what makes a kiss a good one. My eyes meet theirs and they lower their heads. I look away and smile at how much they remind me of myself. I hear one call the other Amoafoa.

Amoafoa. It reminds me of him. And how an imaginary friend turned out to be a full-blown girlfriend, with bones and flesh and blood running through her veins. I try to suppress it, but the laughter bubbles out of me like boiling water.

fear means boy

JOHN

You thought adjusting well to your schedule would be much easier in the second year of university. But no, lecturers like Mr. Banor (with his belly like an overturned boat) insist on giving random quizzes in the middle of the week. So instead of looking forward to red red for lunch, here you are with anxiety in your belly. You look at your phone, and Kwei has sent a message asking if you want your plantain soft or hard. You text back. *Soft. Tell the woman say make she add plenty pepper.*

You're swinging your bag behind you when the light-skinned girl with the long neck and boobs big enough to have a personality of their own calls you *fine boy, no pimple.* You're flattered. But you only have eyes for Baaba. Baaba, whose eyes look like a four-year-old's attempt at drawing pearls—imperfect ovals that slant slightly to the left—with perfect white teeth, skin the color of well-stirred tea, slender as a reed. Every word she speaks rolls out of her mouth like perfectly fried plantain, and when you told her last Friday that you could listen to her talk for twenty-four hours and never get bored, she frowned and asked, "Only twenty-four hours?"

Baaba, with the boyfriend who is so lanky he looks like he could break, who hovers around her like a thirsty determined housefly. Baaba, who you have three-hour late-night conversations with and talk about everything with, from wedgies to dusty roads to A cups to FKA Twigs to existentialism to the relationship between booty rubs and a country's mental well-being. Baaba, who you tell at least once a day, to discourage any friend zoning, that given the opportunity you would press your face into her ass.

There's a queue inside the cafeteria and for a brief second you panic, but then you see Kwei at the back in a peach shirt waving at you and pointing to a table with a tray of food on it. You breathe a sigh of relief and walk towards him.

"You chop already?" You ask him as you ease into the seat.

"I start but I no finish."

"Chale thanks. Like I for join queue before I chop ah anka I go starve."

"I know paa." He laughs at you.

"Mr. Banor say we get quiz, that man we for lash am paa."

"Oh, hahahaha. I know sey e be Wednesday but you go play FIFA?"

"I go come your there for movies but I no go kyer. Momee wants me to do something for her this evening. Next game of FIFA if I win you go write my essay give me."

"*If* you win. If I win too you go do something give me."

"We go see."

You eat hurriedly and head back to class for your last lecture. When lectures are done for the day you meet up with Kwei and walk the ten-minute distance from the school to the junction between the Kpogas furniture shop and Bake Shop Classics, to get a trotro home. You've been friends with Kwei since first year. You met him at the noticeboard, where he was drawing penises on the heads of the newly elected SRC officials, and since then, you guys have made a habit out of walking home daily and singing "*wele, sɛbɛ, kontomire*" to the rhythm of every jiggly ass that walks ahead of you. Not a day passes without him complaining about the dusty stretch of road between the school and the junction. He would look down at his white plimsolls and tell you to look at his feet. How was he supposed to maintain looking fresh if he had to worry about dust every day? He's always in fitted button-down shirts and smelling of semi-expensive cologne, but the girls like it so you can't be mean about it.

You like walking to the junction even though the road turns your black sandals into a rusty metallic zinc. There's a pure-water seller who is always sitting under a tree 300 meters from the school, whose arms look like they were chiseled out of basswood. The signboards on the left side of the street are still littered with red, green, and white campaign posters, displaying bald old men in smocks and suits of the losing party even though elections ended six months ago. The gas station up ahead has a queue of people lining up to buy gas some days, but it's usually empty.

Kwei lives five houses away from you, so you spend most days after class in his house playing FIFA until it's late or until your mother calls you to come eat. He's particular about not eating on his bed; *I no wan see ant for my bed top*, he tells you with a seriousness that fuels you to always have a bag of chips in your backpack. You talk about school and girls and sports—about difficult course subjects and girls you want to shag, and how if you had one, you would readily give your sister to Neymar to marry. The day he reads "supple" off a billboard as "sappla" you laugh so hard he pushes you off the seat next to him.

You like Thursdays because you have only one lecture in the morning, then the rest of the day is dedicated to FIFA. It's 4 p.m. and you've been playing *El Classico* for two hours. Luka Modrić passes to Isco. Kwei bops his head like he already won the match, and you can't wait to wipe the smirk off his dark wood face. With the way you were moving your bodies and jerking the consoles, anyone unfamiliar with the game would assume the two of you were slow learners of a bad dance routine. Your books are in a corner of Kwei's room, against the wall (a cross between a dull yellow and a dirty beige), one sock lying on top of a paperback version of *The Gods Are Not to Blame*.

A charged Messi swiftly passes the ball to Suárez, who delivers a jaw-dropping kick, scoring an equalizer, and laughter tumbles out of your triumphant body. But it's short-lived, because in less than five minutes Cristiano Ronaldo, with his jersey looking like a bride's high heels, is in control; he deftly maneuvers the ball and scores.

Kwei happily bounces on the bed and says "Sosket!" when he wins. You've won four games out of six so far, so you don't know why he's so thrilled. After his excitement dies down, he tells you to close your eyes.

"Why, wosop?"

"I wan show you something. Make you close your eye."

"Small winning you win wey you dey flex like this?" you complain, but you close your eyes. You feel him take the console out of your hand and then place your hands by your side on the bed.

There's silence for a few seconds, then you feel his lips on yours. Tentatively at first, then it progresses into a boldness that gently sucks on your lips.

His lips are soft. Why are they so soft? You can smell him; like a mixture of sweat and that damn aromatic leathery cologne you've learned to identify him by. When his tongue gently parts your lips and dips into your mouth, you hear yourself groan. A soft bellowing sound that makes its way out of your body, as if it's happy to be let out after being held hostage. He interlocks his hand with yours and eases his spare hand gently under your omelette du fromage T-shirt, gently trailing his fingers down your spine, all the way to the swell of your bum. A gasp escapes and you lean forward. He groans so loudly you can feel his body shake against you. His heart thumps so fast you can feel it against your skin. You're not thinking. You can't think. He unbuckles your belt at a hurried pace, fumbles with the metallic buttons till he frees them from the clasp, puts his hand into your jeans and massages with intent and rhythm, and your leg inadvertently jerks forward. Desire snakes through your body as slow as a virus. You don't realize your palms are sweaty until he guides your hand to the swell between his thighs. It is only when you feel his hard-on that you freeze, open your eyes, and pull away.

The room suddenly feels very hot and you're too aware of how loudly the bed creaks when you move. Your scalp prickles and beads of sweat dot your upper lip. You can feel him staring at you but you don't look at him. There's a heavy silence hanging in the room as the embossed adinkra symbol on your sandals becomes a newfound interest, and there's one sentence echoing in your head. *What just happened?*

You're both quiet. It feels like a forced conversation is in progress, but you two are on mute. After what feels like several minutes, you stand to your feet, push the books spilling out of your leather bag back in, almost trip on his worn-out carpet, and make for the door.

"I for go do something for house. I go call you." You walk out without waiting for an answer.

You play the last thirty minutes in your head over and over, tossing and turning and readjusting the striped bedspread repeatedly as though you were rearranging the lines in the design. You look at the familiar squiggly water stain on the ceiling, a remnant of a past relationship between a leaking roof and the rain. And suddenly, your room doesn't bring you as much comfort as it has. You turn things over and over in your chest: the video game, Kwei's lips, the unexplained sprouting of desire, Kwei's erection, your erection; a sharp thing of rage slices through your chest. You're reduced to a madman looking for a linear explanation to remodel you back into the person you knew you were just hours ago.

You're unsure when you fell asleep but your phone vibrating wakes you up. It's Baaba.

"Duuude, why haven't I heard from you in three days?"

You smile. Baaba never says hello.

"Hello, I'm doing very well, thanks for asking. How about you?"

Her laugh spills out of the phone. She asks if she woke you, because you sound like you just woke up, and why are you asleep so early, it's only 12:12 a.m.

"It's 12 a.m.? Damn, I've slept. I came home early today," you tell her.

She asks about lectures and how she's sure a pint of her soul has been squeezed out because she was unlucky to have sat between two fat Ga women in a trotro from Circle to Santa Maria, and you tell her you've spotted some girl in the marketing department with a tiny waist who talks as if there's a whistle lodged in her throat, and you find it funny in a cute way, so you're determined to kiss her to find out if you can borrow the whistle for your throat. It makes her laugh so hard she needs to catch her breath and she calls you a fool. She complains about the stretch marks on her butt, how she was happy to discover them beautifully lined up like eager sprouts two years ago, but it's been two years and her butt is still small. What is the point of stretch marks if they're not going to stretch and make her ass fat like the girl in tourism class with an ass like a speed ramp? You laugh and tell her you're happy that her ass is small because she's already breaking hearts with her face and she wants a big ass on top of all that cuteness? She laughs softly. You can hear her gentle breathing; there's a smile on your face and in that moment you feel content and comfortable and very much yourself.

"Are you okay? You're much quieter today. Everything okay?"

"Kwei kissed me."

Baaba is so surprised she stammers. When you say nothing she asks you softly, as if she's whispering, "John, did you just say Kwei kissed you?"

Silence.

"John, talk to me, please."

You let out a long sigh.

"Kwei kissed me this afternoon. In his room. You know how we always play FIFA on Thursdays and the winner gets to ask the loser for anything? He won one of the games and asked me to close my eyes, and then he kissed me. I don't even know why I'm telling you this, Baaba."

"Don't be silly, of course you can tell me anything." There's an uncomfortable silence, a long one, then she continues.

"Did I ever tell you about Ms. Quarcopoome?"

"Who's that?"

"English teacher from JSS One. That woman is the reason why I'm certain God is unfair. She was so fiiiiine. I didn't even know it was possible to be attracted to someone's legs. If she had told me to close my eyes for a kiss I would've just passed out."

You laugh softly.

"Now tell me what happened?"

"He . . . he just kissed me. He asked me to close my eyes and next thing I know he's kissing me."

"And?"

"And?"

"And what did you do when he kissed you?"

"I, I let him. I didn't pull back. It just happened. I don't know why he kissed me, I don't know why I didn't pull back, and now I don't know what to think. I'm not gay."

"Hey, slow down. Walk me through what happened and what was going through your mind when it happened."

"That's the thing, Baaba. I don't remember thinking. I don't think it would have gone any further if I was think-ing. I've been trying to block it out of my mind since I got home. All I could remember was how incredibly soft his lips were. I never even thought of the possibility of another boy having soft lips. I was turned on. Can you imagine? I was fully turned on. And . . . and he, he touched me. It was only when I felt his dick get hard that I started freaking out."

"Wow."

Your belly tightens in the awkward silence. And you tell

her again that you're not gay. She tells you to stop being silly
and that one kiss with a boy hardly makes you gay.

"Why did I allow the kiss to happen, then, Baaba? That
should have been a 'what the fuck' moment but it never
happened until I felt his dick! I'm here wondering if Kwei is
gay or bi, because his ex is a girl he dated in high school. Even
if he's gay, I'm not mad about it, that's his business. What is
really messing me up right now is why did I not freak out till
way too much had happened? Like? Fuck, man."

She sighs heavily and tells you she doesn't have the answers, but you're working yourself up over nothing. There's
more silence, but you're both lost in your thoughts; you mulling
the event in your head over and over, she mulling over your
recounting of your day's highlight. She tells you about the ridiculousness of a Nollywood sex scene she saw the day before,
and why are Africans always having sex under a bedsheet, can
they even move freely? And you end up talking about movies
for the next thirty minutes until you hear her heavy breathing
and unresponsiveness to the mention of her name.

From nowhere, the exact memory of how Kwei smells
flares up in your mind like a thirst that's not well quenched,
and for five minutes you debate with yourself whether or not
to wake Baaba up to distract you. There's an unglued you that
wants to hate Kwei, punch him even, call him batty boy from
the third floor of the administration block so his humiliation
spreads wide. And there's a you too close for comfort. You remember too vividly the softness of his lips and how easily you
leaned into him like your body had rehearsed it. Suspended

between a feeling of wrongness and rightness, you're so over-whelmed with suffering that you scream into your pillow.

The next day the thought of seeing Kwei in class brings the tightness back to your stomach. So you stay in bed and switch on your laptop, looking for an old series to rewatch. Your mother pokes her head through your door.

"Shouldn't you be getting ready for school? Wo yɛ okay?"

She says it matter-of-factly but there's something about her voice and squint that gives her every word a substance of concern. You mumble something about a headache and how you just need to rest a bit. She drops her bag on the floor and walks to your side, gently presses your neck with the back of her hand, before informing you about the Advil beside the TV stand and the soup in the fridge. She picks up her bag and leaves for work.

You settle on rewatching *The Marvelous Mrs. Maisel*, pleased that it still makes you laugh. Your phone rings after midday. It's Kwei calling. You watch the phone ring until it stops and then you turn your attention back to Mrs. Maisel. He calls you two more times before he gives up. You shove the phone under your pillow and go back to the screen.

When it's 10 p.m. you finally check your phone and there are four messages from Kwei.

At 1:28 p.m.:
Are you not coming to class?

At 3:47 p.m.:
I'm sorry. I don't know what else to say.

At 8:57 p.m.:

The truth? I've been wanting to do that for the past five months. I don't regret it. And maybe it's not right. But I'm sorry. I can't even lie and say I hate myself. I've been looping it in my head since it happened and I would give anything for it to happen again, but not at the expense of our friendship. I'm very sorry, John.

At 9:17 p.m.:

Please say something. I know you can see this.

You delete all his messages and try to fall asleep but the text messages have made you feel worse. He's been wanting to kiss for the past five months?? How did you not notice? He's always been kind to you and does almost anything you ask of him, but so do you! Because he's your friend. That's how friendship works. Or was it something you did or said? Or just too much proximity? So what now? What do you do now? Do you have to confront this? What happens to your friendship now? Should you block him for a bit? Will that help?

You're unhinged. You're at the center of a chaos you didn't ask for. As though someone inside you has betrayed you into limbo and made you a prisoner of confusion.

A week passes by. You do everything in your power to avoid Kwei. His phone calls have reduced but he still calls once a day even though you never pick up. Sometimes you skip school altogether. Or you go to class but you skip lunch and stay in the classroom halls until everyone has left. Sometimes Baaba comes over to eat with you in the old computer lab undergoing refurbishing. On Wednesday she tells you Kwei reached out to her.

"Huh?"

"Yeah. I was leaving the cafeteria when I saw him. I think he had been waiting there for a while. Anyway, John, he asked me if I had seen or spoken to you. If you were okay because he hadn't seen you in school all week and he couldn't reach you via phone. He sounded worried."

"What did you tell him?"

"The truth. That I had seen you, and that you had been to school although you'd also missed some days because you weren't really yourself."

"Oh. Okay."

"John."

"Yeah?"

"You know you can't avoid him forever, right? Are you really mad at him? If you are, then you have to at least have a conversation with him. Completely ignoring him is . . . a little mean. Is that what you want?"

"I'm mostly mad at myself. And I don't mean to be mean, I just don't know what to do. I don't know what to say to him. I just . . . I don't know, Baaba."

Baaba sighs. "Well, I told him to give you a little time, you'd come around. He looked really sad. And I know you're confused about a lot of things, but I think it will help even you, and not just him, if you had a conversation. Even if it's to say that you're confused."

"Mm-hmm."

"Please, think about it."

"Okay."

"Promise?"

"I'll think about it."

"All right."

Another week passes by. You're moody and quiet and sleeping so much it alarms even you. Your mother keeps asking if you're okay, asks why you're acting like someone died, did anybody die? You keep telling her you're fine while lying in bed all day and barely eating. On Friday she tells you she needs a favor; could you take a package to your uncle K's house in Ada? It's a two-hour journey from your house, so you ask her if you can leave early morning on Saturday. You leave at 5 a.m. and get there a few minutes after 7. Uncle K is just about to leave Ada for Accra on an emergency. He asks you if you can stay till the next day; he had rented one of his two units to a man for the weekend, and needed someone to be around in case the man needed anything. You agree to stay, you were tired anyway and, luckily for you, your Monday morning class had been postponed to 2 p.m., so you could leave back for Accra late Sunday and still get some rest before you headed for class. You fell asleep instantly.

A rather loud playing of Bon Iver's "Heavenly Father" wakes you up in the evening. You're sure it's Uncle K's guest but you go out just to be sure. A large dark-skinned man is stretched out on the porch with a speaker at his left side. He notices you and asks if he just woke you up or if you're out because you love the music. You tell him both, he laughs, tells you his name is Mike, and pats the ground next to him. He tells you he came here just so he can listen to his two-hour playlist without having to change diapers or attend to a crying toddler. Next week is his wife's turn. After more than an hour you know all about his life in uni, how he hates driving, and the black lipstick his wife loves so much. You think his initiative to ban men from wearing boxer shorts is hilarious and ridiculous, and you think his admitting to not really liking his two-year-old son is a scary thing for a father to say. It's only been a little over an hour of speaking with him, but you haven't laughed this much and felt this free in the last two weeks.

"Yo so, Mike, random but I want your opinion and possibly advice for a friend of mine."

"Yeah? I'm listening."

"So we'll call this friend of mine Kojo. Kojo is friends with another guy who we will call Tony. They're very good friends, they've been friends for a year or so now. They have a routine of sorts, where they spend Thursdays playing FIFA. On one of the Thursdays out of nowhere, Tony kissed Kojo. Kojo may have been slow to stop the kiss but he eventually did. And now he is a mess of emotions. He's upset and confused and sad. And wondering if he may be gay."

"Whoa. Slow down. Tony kissed Kojo. Kojo is upset—fair. Why is Kojo wondering if he may be gay."

"Chale, I don't know. But I think Kojo is thinking this way because he didn't immediately stop the kiss. It might have lingered for a while before he stopped it."

"Ahh. I see. Hmm. Well. I don't know much about homo-sexuality but I think that if a man is able to picture himself penetrating or being penetrated by another dude, then he's likely gay. But if he's unable to hold that imagery, he's prob-ably not. But you know the honest truth? I don't understand why Ghanaian men are so uptight about what another man chooses to do with his body. Me, for instance, I like it very much when my wife gently strokes the line in between my butt cheeks. And I can bet on the government's bloated parliament that more than a handful of men do too."

You snort through your nose.

"See, I get the hostility around homosexuality in this country. We have taken religion world cup in this country. But chale, my God asks more for me to love my fellow human than to crucify him, you know?"

Mike's phone rings. "Wifey is calling. I'll be back."

"Cool cool."

You lie there thinking about the conversation you just had. Just speaking the words out loud feels relieving, but hearing him say all that has done something for you.

You don't remember how long you stayed lying there by yourself. You don't remember how the easiness shifted itself around your chest, you don't remember if it was gradual or circuitous or instant, but it felt like finally being able to breathe through a blocked nose. You finger your phone cautiously. Two weeks is a long time to reply to a text message.

drip

AYELEY

"Away!" The bus conductor shouts as he slaps the side of the white trotro after a man with a beige hat has squeezed into the last available seat. The driver starts the ignition, the car shudders, and then he drives off. On the side of the road, a small market stretches out, dotted by loud women seated behind pans of fresh fish, screaming out for customers and swatting flies away simultaneously.

He veers off the main road and turns into an untarred road. "I dey swerve traffic small," he says, turning briefly to the passengers before turning his eyes back onto the road. He passes by a KVIP, and the unmistakable scent of collective shit rises like smoke. The houses we drive past have rusty roofs and windows with missing louvres and blue fading walls that look like water seeped into a drawing.

As we reach the end of the street, a low guttural voice behind me starts humming a Presbyterian hymn. I recognize it because my grandmother is always singing it.

The woman who sits two seats ahead of me wears a navy-blue T-shirt that reads *Caro made me do it*. She looks as if she is thinking long and hard about something important, with her partly squinted eyes and folded lips. She holds the bottom of her phone closer to her mouth, speaking slowly. There is something about her voice that reminds me of Mary Ann, a girl from secondary school with a voice that could put a congregation to sleep, whose school mother told all the seniors on our block, who went ahead and told everybody else in the boardinghouse, that she caught her masturbating at dawn. I wonder if navy-blue T-shirt has ever touched herself before. I wonder if she has ever touched herself in the backseat of an empty car. I wonder if the act of touching yourself in open spaces constitutes waywardness, or something completely abominable. A teenager with breasts three times bigger than mine blocks my view. I imagine myself as a teenager, with no breasts, and figuring out life for myself, and I think this teenager will be just fine. She's wearing a red faux leather skirt that exposes a creamy thigh with two beauty spots lined up on it, as if God placed them there as an afterthought. Tiny beads of sweat are covering her nose. She's gesturing wildly and telling someone on the phone that a boy called Kpakpo is a big fat liar because she, Akwele, has never read Mills & Boons or any sex novels, she only reads correct books and has even started reading John Grisham. We're on the highway now and the driver is speeding like he's being chased. The previously trapped hot air is replaced with a gush of wind that slightly suffocates me. The wind swallows parts of the teenager's conversation and I struggle to keep up, but when she says the word *sex*, it lights up the trotro in a flash. When she says *sex*, it feels to me like popping a toffee into your mouth, only to discover after the first bite that it is bitter kola. She looks sixteen or seventeen, with large eyes and a big lower lip, and I still think she will do just fine if she does not grow into another year not knowing what comes after a body is developed and desire rents space in it. When lust tiptoes into her veins on random Sunday afternoons. And she discovers the desire to lie with a man who will have no regard for his fleeting feelings for her. And all the phone calls she has made and the "correct" books she has read are pushed aside and forgotten. When they make no difference to the men she will come to love who will then come to leave her. The man sitting next to her is fixated on his phone, and somehow his elbow presses into the side of her boob. She gives him a look that could peel the flesh off fingers.

I'm transported back to being nine years old and in class 3. When my class teacher, Mr. Akwetey, shuffled the class and arranged the seating order such that no two boys or girls were sitting close to each other, every girl had to sit next to a boy and vice versa. I was already sulking at the prospect of having to be in class 3 again, I was supposed to be in class 4, but when I passed my entrance test in the last town my father was posted to, they thought I was smart enough to be in class 3 instead of class 2. But since we came back to the city my father thought it would be good for me to be with my age mates. So here I was stuck in a class I had already been in and sitting by Larry with the big head and lazy eyes. I had wanted to sit by the girl with the Barbie band in her hair but I was stuck with Larry. And even though he was too fidgety for a boy his age he shared his Super 2 biscuits with me at lunch, so it wasn't so bad. One day during handwriting class, he took my hand from underneath the table and guided it to the front of his brown pants. His zipper was open and the unexpectedness of skin caused me to hit my foot against the table. Mr. Akwetey was painstakingly writing out *the big brown fox jumps over the lazy dog* in cursive handwriting on the blackboard. I looked up to see if anybody could see what was happening underneath the table. I looked back at Larry. He turned his attention to the blackboard and kept his hold on my wrist, moving my hand in a to-and-fro movement around his genitals. I felt frozen, but I did not whisk my hand away. And then he pulled my skirt a little further up with his left hand and urgently pushed his fingers through. After class I stayed in my seat and refused to go for lunch even though I was dying for a strawberry lollipop. I hid my hand in my pocket and didn't take it out till my father picked me up from school.

I changed my seat the next day, and even though Larry offered me half his lunch and Super 2, even though Mr. Akwetey made me kneel for an hour for taking Baafi's seat, I refused to go back to my seat and sat in Baafi's for the next three days until Mr. Akwetey finally gave up. I would think often about this incident and be filled with crippling guilt; swallowing down questions and willing the act to absolve me of my guilt. I wondered if I was a good child, and if I was, had this one sin revoked my goodness? Should I have taken my hand off? Did staying still imply my willingness? Was there anything I did to invite him to touch me that day? Did I subconsciously want to touch him? Should I have told someone about this?

In class 4, my father was transferred to a church outside the city, so we moved out, and I never saw Larry again.

A strong smell hits my nose and I glance accusingly at the man sitting beside me. If you can fart in an enclosed space then you can buy your own car and fart every ten minutes. I am glad to get off at the next stop.

Taking my clothes off when I get home is a hurried ritual, as if the rest of my sanity depends on how fast I can unhook my bra. The mirror repeats every action back to me and when I look it straight in the eye, I think that it is fair to say that, me too I be fine girl. Ink dey for my body small. My hair is impractically tough but somehow I'm able to tame it. Clothes fall easily on my sides with no hips to distract them. I have had lovers tell me they love me even though I have no breasts, as though I should be thankful to them for their attraction towards me despite my orange breasts. I have had them explore my body with their fingers as though they were intent on looking for a treasure by digging just on the surface. I have seen pleasure leaking out of them like vapor, winced at how long I housed the idea that my own body—all women bodies—were incapable of courting pleasure.

Once, in the bathroom of a four-star hotel, Naana and

I spent thirty-two minutes trying to draw perfect eyebrows on for Yasmin's twenty-third birthday. We had been friends for four years. I met her at a Spiritual Union camp telling a boy that he couldn't laugh at a girl for being an A cup when he had the smallest feet. We bonded instantly. We liked the same movies, and were both mean to boys. Snapchat was the cool thing then and we took pleasure in not being cool kids. We'd written and directed a one-minute film titled *Girls on Snapchat Be Like* . . . And she'd once walked closely behind me from the mall to get a taxi just so nobody else could see the bloodstain on my skirt. She was unfiltered and unapologetic about it.

"How often do you masturbate?" She dabbed the tip of her left eyebrow with her pinky finger.

I blinked and looked at her for a second too long. Her question threw me off guard. I swallowed hard and shifted uncomfortably.

"Um, I don't masturbate."

"What? Are you serious?"

"Yeah . . ."

"Ah, Ayeley, you're joking. Not even dry humping? Sweet baby Jesus!"

She placed the brown eye pencil on the marble sink and turned to me.

"Listen to me. Touch yourself. Touch yourself, you hear? How do you give someone permission to travel a road you've not used yourself? How do you expect the trip to be smooth when you don't know how to get there? Do not let another man visit the Promised Land when you haven't graced the walls of the land with your holiness."

Later, I would pull out this conversation from my memory, sit with it, sleep with it, wake up to it, and unpack the meaning from it.

I remember Madam Rita from Sunday school telling us that masturbation is a sin. I remember Pastor Michael, stiff necked and eyes wide, telling us how masturbation done alone and accompanied by lust is a grave sin. I remember Fred telling a group of girls that God is deeply sad whenever we go against his word and give in to the flesh, and I wonder how anybody could feel that way when there is an urgent thread of desire pushing itself out of a body, when pleasure is bonding with relief and hugging itself around my toes. I remember Aunty Jasmine threatening to tell Mommy when she saw me with my hand in my crotch on the couch after school.

I remember discovering what my body was capable of. How I never loved my body until I touched myself. I slide my fingers down in a pleasing manner, imitating an ardent lover, imagining a wanton partner, the buzz and eagerness to please, the careless affection.

I slide my underwear out of the way and rock my finger to and fro. And then as the intensity builds up, as the seemingly long spurt of excitement announces itself, as it ushers in its promise of glorious release, I part my chapped lips, only ever so slightly, swallowing quick and hard, and I think of how alive this makes me feel—and then I let it drip.

Gen Y ♀ Sexual Behavior

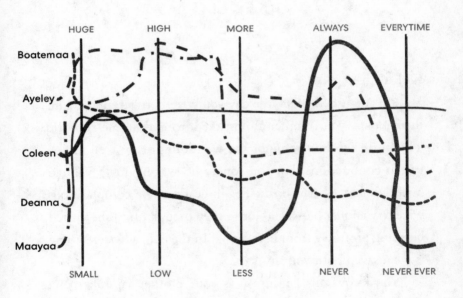

stubborn anyway

KEKELI

Kekeli

On August 18, 1994, the day you were born, around 2 a.m. thereabouts, your mother almost died from a uterine rupture. The nurse on duty thought she was doing really well in between contractions. For someone who was having a vaginal birth after a cesarian birth, her indications for complications were few and far between—or so they thought until she started bleeding profusely from her vagina. In the end, a hysterectomy is what saved both your lives.

You know this because it is your mother's number one point of reference for emotional blackmail.

"I almost died having you, Kekeli! Next to the blood of Jesus that saved us is the blood I lost in delivering you! Why is the kitchen looking like you don't have home training? Are you trying to kill me again, Keli?"

Whether it was threat or praise, you were always reminded that your mother almost died giving birth to you.

Her Presbyterian women's choir voice is a sound that breaks out in your head without permission.

Sometimes you think that you would love your mother so much better if she were a distant memory. You imagine her dead sometimes, a memory spun from the generous copies of photographs in the seven stacks of albums under the coffee table in the living room, tracing your fingers over her sepia-toned face at twenty-one years old, wearing a white sailor playsuit and ridiculous pointy shoes, a memory made solid by your father's sandpaper voice repeating fantastic stories about her over and over. It's a thought you can never entertain for long because your very alive mother either yells out your name or calls your phone if you're not two feet away from her. It's as if her spirit can hear your careless thoughts and immediately calls you to put a stop to that nonsense.

Sibi

All they show on the TV these days are sex scenes. The sun is still hot and children are returning home from school, all kinds of intimacy on TV. They won't even wait till 10 p.m. Why? The movies are not bad, I just don't understand why it has to be 2 p.m. This Majid Michel movie with a kissing scene every ten minutes, they've shown it at least three times ahba! I like that movie. It reminds me of Kudzo and I before the children came.

We used to joyously rock our hips even more after marriage. Marriage validated our sex life and turned us into horny bats. We both wanted three children. He wanted two boys and one girl. I wanted two girls and one boy. Fate had other plans. Selorm would've been an easy delivery had he not decided to come three weeks early and in breech position. The doctors said it was absolutely necessary to have a cesarean. Kekeli came three full years after him, and I thought, finally, I can now push, so that when other women are speaking of the pains of childbirth, I too can call myself woman. The pool of blood that left my body when birthing that child, it is a wonder I did not die. But it was scary enough for Kudzo and I to decide that she was our last child.

When Kekeli was born, she was a copy of her father. The same blasé eyes and a traffic cone for a nose. I swear! But over the years her face has changed to accommodate my genes. She has my Dagbani monolid eyes, perpetually shiny forehead, half-doughnut cheeks. And my distinct black upper lip and bright pink lower lip have marked their territory on her face. It delights me to no end! She was her father's sunshine. She was the sum of all the daughters I wanted to have. She was my good thing. And so we named her Kekeli Daliri Fiator.

Ah? This same Majid Michel movie again? Has TV3 run out of movies or something? Where is the remote?

"Kekeli! Kekeli, are you downstairs?"

What good is a good thing if she cannot come all the way upstairs to change an ordinary TV channel?

"Kekeli! Kekeli! Come and help me find the remote, my dear."

Kekeli

You're halfway through brushing your teeth when you hear the phone ring. You gurgle and rinse. Caller ID is Selorm with two black heart emojis next to the name. Your heart sinks a little. You love your brother to death but right now what you need is for Eugene to call you back. You called and sent him a message at 6:07 a.m.; how busy was he that he still hadn't gotten back to you at 9:54 a.m.? He wasn't busy when he lied to his boss so he could get off work at 2 p.m. to see you. He wasn't busy when you used the money your dad gave you on your birthday for a white lingerie set because he said your skin made the color white look like royalty. He wasn't busy all the nights you spent with him in his warm-as-shit room. But *now* he's too busy to call you back? Boys are so full of shit. You wish you could talk to Selorm. You wish you had told him the minute it began that you were seeing his best friend. He would have been firmly against it and you would've gone ahead anyway but at least it wouldn't be alien to him now and you could've spoken to him. Selorm has always known what to say, if only you could tell him. The ringing ends before you can hit the answer button.

If you are a somewhat adequate mash-up of both parents, your brother Selorm is a clone of your father. They have the exact same face—deep-set eyes, protruding nose, and full lips. They even have the same birthmark at the back of their necks, and they both squint when they're angry.

When you were small the two of you used to sneak into the kitchen and lick leftover pepper till your tongues hung outside your mouths and begged for freedom. Once, he got into a fight with a boy who spat on you because he wanted to see how far his spit could travel from the library on the second floor to the tuck shop downstairs. And he did lose the fight, but that didn't stop him from spitting into the boy's water bottle every day at break till the term ended. Selorm was very protective of you. You did everything together. Whether it was football or homework or washing dishes or playing ampe. You wanted to be brave and daring like him. You wanted to be just like him. You even thought you would grow a penis like him at some point. And so imagine your shock and betrayal when, a month after you turned twelve, your period plopped into your favorite sky-blue panties. Shock that quickly turned into tears and anger, because you knew without a doubt that you were going to be in this body forever. How you sat on the bathroom floor and sobbed loudly as your too-happy-to-see-your-period mother tried to console you. And how quickly her face changed when you asked her if there was still a chance you could grow a penis like Selorm's.

It was the first time your mother shrank away from you in disappointment.

You think of that often, of how disbelief clouded her face, how she leaped away from you on the floor like you were a disease she didn't want to catch. How she went calling for your father to come listen to "his daughter," as though she couldn't believe this girl sprang out of her body.

You think of that now, and you wonder if, perhaps, you are not the daughter your mother bargained for. That you cause her so much disappointment from resisting what she considers to be for your good.

Your phone rings again.

Sibi

I got my first period when I was ten. I was bent over the stony slab grinding dried pawpaw seeds when Maa started clapping from the corner of the room. She pointed to the stain in my dress and happily danced away to tell my father his daughter was turning into a woman. I didn't understand any of this, burst into tears, ran into the shared bathroom, and refused to come out.

After some coaxing Maa brought me out of the bathroom and gave me a boiled egg. Told me not to bite into it but to swallow it whole. Of course I bit into it. Have you seen how small my mouth is?

Maa swore that if I bit into the egg I would be eating my unborn child. That didn't work.

She threatened to not let me into the house until I had swallowed it. That didn't work either.

She threatened to lash me with cane soaked in cold water overnight. After three eggs, and a combination of threats, I finally swallowed an egg. She danced around me all evening. At supper, I got the biggest meat. Even bigger than Papa's. That evening she sat me down and told me that I was now a woman; before, there was no difference between me and the boys in the playground, but now, with my period, my body had undoubtedly announced itself as a woman to the world.

I have always wanted to do the same for my Keli. When she was ten and her period hadn't come, I thought it might have been because she was well fed. These things are tricky; sometimes good living delays the inevitable. When she was eleven and still no blood, I knew it was because of her father's blood. Ėvēs are stubborn.

When she turned twelve, I heard her crying in her room: blood from down there had stained her favorite panties, she said. Finally! What joy! Was it new cotton panties that she needed? I had been saving a fresh pair for this day. I rushed off to boil an egg for her. Boiled three, just in case, you know, she was like her mother.

But no. This one was nothing like her mother.

Cried herself sore. I didn't understand any of it. Knocked the egg away and told me she wanted a penis like her brother's. The crying I understood. It is distressing to wake up one day and be bleeding from your lady parts, and then to be told it is a normal thing that you should expect every single month. Even I, with all my mother's infectious joy, cried about my period when it showed up. But wanting to grow a penis?? A GIRL GROWING A PENIS??? Where did that come from? Who told her she could? Why does she even want to? What's wrong with her body and how was I finding this out now?

"I don't want to menstruate, I want some of Selorm's penis."

Girls have cried. Girls have hidden in dark corners. Girls have been afraid, even. But no girl has wanted a penis in place of a period. What was I to do? Nobody prepares you for this stuff.

Kekeli

It was the way your mother's voice swelled into a high pitch whenever she asked or talked to you about you being unemployed that made you nervous. Like she couldn't believe you still didn't have a job. Like your time was running out. Like she was more worried about you not being employed than you were about it. Of course you were worried; you had a tall list of things you would buy the minute you got your first salary. But what hadn't you done? If you assembled all the printed copies of your CV you've dropped off at companies you could sell it to the groundnut seller. You've been in so many interviews, the mere mention of the word *interview* made you dizzy. You could be at home all the time but her anxiety about your unemployment made you anxious so you spent most days out of the house.

Walking into the kitchen to get the pineapple you sliced last night, you hear her laughter before you see her. Her legs are folded underneath her, elbows sinking into a pillow for support. She's watching something on the TV. You tell her her green-and-peach dress is matching with the Jesus picture hanging above the TV. She smiles and tells you to come watch TV with her.

You obey because it's the one place you both agree. The one moment there's less tension.

Sibi

Me and Kekeli are watching a telenovela when Maria the maid starts vomiting, so I tell Keli she must be pregnant.

"Is that how pregnant women act? Puking all the time?"

"Yes. Especially in your first trimester."

"Oh, okay."

"Maria's madam's son has been playing around with her, so I won't be surprised if we find out she's pregnant. If she is, trouble."

"She's very pretty."

"Saa eh? Pretty won't save you in the real world o. Pretty will just let men disturb you. If you want your peace of mind as a woman you have to have your own job, something you do for yourself, and then you find a good man to marry you, and then you can get pregnant."

"Okay . . ."

"I'm just saying. I know you already know this but that's the way it should be. Anyway, I'm not worried. We raised you well. Not like Cynthia's daughter, who I hear has two kids now and is still unmarried. Not one o. Two kids! Her eldest is six years old and that girl is your age. God forbid. Not my child. Never."

"But . . . what has that got to do with what we're watching?"

"I'm just saying o."

Kekeli

The last place you want to be is at a trotro station. Too many people, too many strange hands touching you for no reason other than to ask if you are going to Kasoa or Lapaz. Dirt and sweaty armpits and wayside food competing for space. But a trotro is what you can afford since you used all your money on three stupid hospital tests because you can never be sure of store-bought pregnancy kits. You look at your phone for the umpteenth time.

Your mother texts instead. She's saved okro soup for you in an ice cream bowl for when you get back home, and there's banku in the ice chest on top of the small fridge. Your frown uncoils into a big smile. She knows banku and okro is your favorite. In that instant you almost want to call her and tell her everything. But you push it down and walk towards the Labadi buses.

There are only six people in the bus, so you're able to secure a window seat. In less than fifteen minutes the bus is full and the driver is heading for the main road. A post-office-blue 207 Benz bus passes by your bus and you could've sworn it was one of Dada's cars if it weren't for the "I told you so" inscription and the Action Chapel sticker on the back.

In 2006, Dada took a bank loan to start a transport business. He bought ten blue 207 Benz buses and hired twenty-one people: ten drivers, ten mates, and one manager/accountant. All the cars had "God is good" inscribed on the back. Often during morning devotion, your mother would ask everyone to "pray for *God is good* ventures, for God to make it big."

By 2008, Dada had added nine more cars and joined the Ghana Private Road Transport Union. He made enough money to buy a house in Taifa, and start building one in his home-town. The house in Taifa was a picture out of the seventies. Someone had planted bougainvillea in the shape of a C that shrouded the house and gave it a calm about itself. The walls were made up of stones stacked on top of each other, jutting from each other in the right places.

But the best part about Taifa came from your neighbor Auntie Abena and her sons. She had an eight-year-old son and a seventeen-year-old son who was away at boarding school— she would make condense toffee and shito every other weekend to be sent to the security man, who would pass it on to her son.

She would stir milk and a chunk of butter until it was golden brown. You loved watching her spread it on a chopping board, roll deftly, and cut it into little chunks. Sometimes she would let you roll them. But it was eating the toffee that you loved the most.

You would lick the sweet golden brown toffee until the back-and-forth motion had worn out your tongue, and only then would you sink your teeth into the sponginess of it, and proceed to spend minutes pulling chunks of it out of your teeth. You got to send some of it home. You knew you weren't supposed to eat from strangers, but it was so good. Plus, this didn't really count as food. It was just caramel toffee. And you loved it. You looked forward to Saturdays. You craved the smooth sweetness of it. You would endure the ordinary taste of food piously in anticipation of a faithful licking. You had found something to love. You had finally latched on to a wanting.

Until your mother found out about the toffees.

She called you an ungrateful child. Eating other people's food like you had never been fed. Was it because of condense toffee that you had turned into a beggar? Not even for the sake of fancy food her tongue could not pronounce, condense toffee! How could you? She never did such a thing to her own mother. Why did you, Kekeli Daliri Fiator, want to bring disgrace unto the family's name?

You shriveled, fear thawing in your bones, caramel melting in your pocket.

It lasted for weeks. Your mother's hurt has always had a long lifespan. And so her disdain bled through days. Every sentiment reeked of undertones of shame. She rubbed it in your face at the dinner table: "Lord, may this food be as sweet as Auntie Abena's toffees so wandering feet can stay planted." You felt it in the way she refused to let you help her with washing the dishes. In the way she dragged her eyes over you whenever you forgot yourself and laughed at something funny she had said. Until finally during supper your father spoke sharply: "Are you still on this thing, Sibiri? Ahn ahn. So who is the child here? Let the girl rest."

She let it go, but you were never forgiven for wanting.

The phone vibrates in your pocket. Eugene finally.

Sorry for the late reply, we had a work meeting that I couldn't get away from. I just sent money to your account, Keli. We have to do this. We *need* to do this. Please. I'm stuck at work, I'll call you as soon as I can.

You grind your teeth and attempt to crack all ten knuckles but it hurts on your little finger. You want to punch something. Anything. But you're stuck in a trotro.

Sibi

Children never listen to you. They think they know better. They think you must hate them because you won't allow them to do whatever they want. Am I supposed to look on while she makes stupid mistakes that will cost her enormously?

For someone who is unemployed Kekeli always has somewhere to be. I never know where she goes to or what she's doing. She claims she's job searching but not once has she actually gotten any of the jobs she's gallivanting about for. And all this for what? Almost twenty-five and still jobless. If she had listened to me and studied nutrition or biology or any of the sciences, she could have easily been a doctor, or even a nurse. Or anything, even! Because we all know that the only thing this country respects is a science degree. But no, it had to be performing arts. Why does the university even have that department? What job exists for these students? In this country? Does the country even have a theater besides that white elephant of a National Theatre?

I don't even get this education thing. I didn't even get to go to university, but at twenty-five I was already working and looking after Maa and Daa. But this one is always collecting feeding money, transport money, money for clothes, money for this, money for that, and oh, Mummy, I'm still looking for a job, I've sent my CV everywhere. What is all this? Kudzo does not take her unemployment seriously, telling me not to worry, she will eventually find one, and we have raised her well enough to find a good husband. How? My Keli will not be a burden to anyone. I need her to find a job.

This Mr. Amot, I have sent Keli's CV to him three times, but he is still not telling me any proper thing. How can you be a whole CEO and you can't even help place one graduate? Ghanaians will just give themselves titles for no reason. When Kudzo comes home this evening we have to start thinking of something else, because Keli has to work soon. I'm worried. She's been home for too long.

It is so dark outside and I know this girl is not taking a taxi; what is she doing out that she is not home by 9 p.m.?

Kekeli

You remember Saturday, May 16, 2009, like a bad movie scene. Mckenzie Otu, the youth pastor's younger brother, came over so the two of you could watch *Indiana Jones and the Kingdom of the Crystal Skull*. He spilled Coca-Cola on the sofa and amid his rambling of an apology, you both frantically tried to squeeze the liquid out of the brown polyester sofa with your cupped hands.

I'm so sorry, I'm so distracted. You're sooo painfully pretty.

Giggling. You point to the Coke stain on his green shirt. He tries to wipe it and makes it worse with his already stained hands. More giggling. You reach for a napkin to wipe it off. Your hands touch. It feels electric. He leans in and plants his lips on yours. You don't know what to do with your tongue but his is rummaging through your mouth. You don't know what to do with your hands but his find their way underneath your blouse. They're squeezing as if they aren't breasts, as if they're ripe fruits at Kaneshie market. They're trying to get . . . somewhere . . . left breast? Both breasts? Oh . . . Bra comes loose, he found a nipple and moaned inside your mouth. It's hard to concentrate. His tongue is still rummaging in your mouth, but with more saliva. You still don't know what to do with your hands. Are you supposed to touch his nipp—

"Kekeli!! Jesus Christ of Nazareth. Oh, Yehowah. This girl will kill me. This girl will take me to my grave. What did I do to deserve this, Father Lord?"

She was supposed to be at choir practice. Which didn't end until way after 6 p.m.

Mckenzie was given a dressing down. She addressed him like she was a delegation sent from God. Asked him if that was what his parents taught him. Told him he ought to be ashamed of himself, assured him his parents would be hearing about this, and asked him to go home right away. The entire time you kept your eyes glued to the floor as you waited for your own dressing down. Instead she sat on the sofa and cried as if she had just found out you had a chronic disease. The next day your mother woke up early so she could go report you to the youth pastors. You were silent until you realized she meant it. You cried yourself sore. Refused to wear church clothes. Selorm was in his school hostel and you called him to make her stop. She turned her phone off and refused to talk to anybody. Selorm called and tried to calm you down. Told you to be apologetic instead of crying because it would just infuriate her, and your mother was just doing this because she wanted the best for you. You begged Dada to stop her.

It will never happen again, I swear!

I cAn't hElp yOu this tImE, kEli, yOu'rE nOt evEn EigHtEen aNd You'rE BrInGiNg bOyS tO tHiS hOuSe.

Nothing and no one could stop her.

In church, she made you sit directly in front of the pulpit. Pastor Michael's sermon was on "keeping ourselves for Christ." It felt like he and your mother had met the night before and plotted sermon notes. He cautioned the entire youth congregation to abstain from premarital sex and masturbation, and engaging in anything that would lead them into temptation. *We would be sinning against God and our own bodies.* The whole time he was looking at you. You felt wretched and defeated. You didn't feel like you belonged to yourself. Mckenzie did not come to church.

After church, your mother went up to Pastor Michael to thank him, and then fetched you from the front and whisked you away. There were no boys allowed home for a very long time. You never forgave your mother for wanting perfection more than she wanted you.

Sibi

"Kudzo, what will you eat? It's just you and me and Keli. Selorm is not coming home this weekend.

"I still have some leftover kontomire stew, so some rice

with that should do. I think Selorm said that he and Eugene have some overtime to do in the office.

"Ahhh, at least you know that your son has a good boy from a good home for a best friend. So you don't have to worry too much. Plus, he's a man, he can take care of himself. By the way, have you called your school friend? The one who can help with the job for Kekeli? Or will you send his number so I can speak to him?

"Oh yes yes, Martin Klu, I was waiting for a good time to call. I think I'll call him right after I'm done speaking to you, and then probably you could call him later in the evening as well.

"All right. See you soon.

"Hello, Martin, this is Sibiri. Kudzo's wife. He asked me to call you.

"Yes o, we are all fine. Everybody is doing well by the grace of God.

"Yes, yes. How are you and the family? And Mrs. It's been such a long time, we have to visit soon.

"We thank God, we thank God.

"Yes, yes, it's about Keli. Yes, Kekeli.

"Hahaha, she's a big girl now. Very very smart too.

"Errm, she did theater but she can fit anywhere o, Martin, she is very smart o, I'm not even saying this because she's my daughter. She's very good, she was top of her class.

"Yes! You know, she has my green fingers and she has her father's brains, so everything is perfect. She's too good, she will do so well wherever you place her.

"Hahaha, oh Martin, I'm being honest, she's a smart kid.

"Mm-hmm. Mm-hmm. Yes.

"She can start anytime, she's been ready to work since since. Just give me a date and she will show up.

"Yes.

"Hahaha.

"Thank you so much, Martin, she will be there. I will have her call you.

"Thank you. I will tell Kudzo. My regards to Mrs.

"Buh-bye."

Kekeli

"I cannot go alone, Eugene.

"Are you saying you can't take a day off? Not even a half day?

"No. No. I don't want to go by myself. I can't.

"We. Say 'we.' Stop saying 'you' like this is on just me.

"I cannot go alone, Eugene.

"If we're getting rid of this then we're doing it together?

"I know, but I'm scared.

"They close at 6 p.m., what if I booked an appointment for four? Would you be able to take time off then?

"Eugene, I'm so scared.

"I'm trying to stop crying but . . .

"My mother can't know.

"Okay, so I go for an early morning appointment with Grace then I'll wait at Grace's place for you?

"Can you make it earlier? If you can come at two or even one.

"Okay."

Kekeli

It's been eight and a half weeks now since you last had your period. You didn't know you were pregnant until the fifth week, and even then, you didn't believe it. You're irritable and bloated and bewildered at how nauseated you feel. This morning before you left the house you wore an oversized jean jacket because you were terrified of your mother spotting your swollen breasts. You think fear is a tummy ache that never gets better. It doesn't diminish, just further diffuses. Moves from your belly at the possibility of pregnancy, wiggles its way to your chest when you and your boyfriend decide that the only way out is to get rid of it, bolts to your throat when you realize he's given every excuse to avoid being in the same room as you since you found out, breaks out into dread when you think of your mother ever finding out, reaches your toes when you wish you could tell somebody. Anybody.

Besides the queuing you had to do even though you had an appointment time, Marie Stopes didn't smell so bad. Hospitals made you nauseated. But instead of the strong smell of disinfectant, the waiting area smelled like a combination of antacids and bubble gum. The girl sitting across from you mindlessly shakes her right leg. The continuous movement of her leg triggers a restlessness in you. Or maybe you were already restless. Everything irks you: having to wait thirty-six minutes and counting to see a doctor, your joblessness, your mother, your body for getting pregnant, Eugene, your inability to buy the things you wanted to buy, the fact that you'd been spending all your time in the library in the last two weeks just to avoid your mother finding out you're pregnant, your brother for being friends with Eugene, the awful nausea brewing inside.

The girl ahead of you is called in to see a doctor. A short dark-skin girl walks into the waiting area. Behind her is a tall skinny man holding what appears to be her bag in his armpit. You watch as he treats her with tenderness, rubbing her back, touching her face, speaking softly to her, and holding her hand.

A fresh wave of rage enters you. It wasn't that you wanted to keep this baby. Of course you weren't ready for one. Your unemployed ass had less than 1,000 cedis in your account; how could you be ready for a baby? In Sibiri Fiator's house? So she wails like her world has ended and accuses you of trying to kill her?

It was that you felt painfully alone. Discarded. Abandoned. Purposefully ignored.

"Kekeli Daliri Fiator?"

"Yes."

"Please come."

things mother will never know

mother wants me to face
each day with a smile
and a gait more pious than Jesus's
how do I tell her my heart
is breaking because a boy woke up
one day and fell out of love with me
like wonky legs falling into gutters?
When I was 7 a family ~~friend~~ sat me
on his ~~crotch~~ crotch and swayed along
to hot cross buns
I didn't learn how to kiss well till I was 24
I didn't enjoy sex till I was 27
horniness wakes me up at dawn
I too have broken someone's heart
When she blesses me with long life
I do not throw my head back
and laugh at Sheol calling my name
I sink into her palm
and receive it with a smile

patchwork

NANA KWEKU OPOKU AGYEMANG JNR.

The market next to the old Ghana Telecoms office is carpeted by a patchwork of sounds.

"Yeeeeiisss, kosua ne moko fressshhh, wodi baako wo bedi mienu." The egg seller's piercing voice cuts through; the chortle of a deep-voiced tomato seller trying to convince a customer to buy her bucket of smashed tomatoes and the whine of a woman wearing a floral dress with a push-up bra that is doing a little too much to her bosom, determined to get a discount from abochi.

Abochi with his forced laughter strikes his butcher's knife against the raised wooden slab, swiftly and effortlessly cutting up two pounds of reddish goat meat into little chunks. The authority of Auntie Adisa's macho voice as she tries to bully a passerby into paying two times the cost for accidently kicking her pail of amane onto the ground. Feet being reluctantly dragged, hurried steps, paced walking to the tune of a tempo only the walkers can hear.

But it's not the egg seller's loud self-announcement that catches your attention, it's her plaid shirt. You've been looking for a plaid shirt with just those colors for the longest time. Blocks of navy blue and navy green intersecting with thin pink stripes; just the perfect color combination that compliments her leather-black skin, and will do justice to your charcoal-black skin. You try to avoid her look, because the minute that eye contact happens, you're going to have to buy boiled egg with hot pepper cushioned in its belly. And we all know she's right when she says once you eat one you'll have to eat two. Boiled egg and pepper does that to you.

The ground is soft from yesterday. The rains were not heavy enough to create muddy pools and temporary sinking grounds, neither were they light enough to dry after the sun went up. The vegetable stall looks like a Crayola palette. Neatly arranged rows of green and red pepper, like 9-to-5ers who methodically form long queues at trotro stations every morning. White fat onions bumping heads with a gathering of light brown onions, looking like a party in power and the opposing party in parliament. Healthy-looking green peas bundled together in sets of ten and fifteen sit beside modest-looking rows of garden eggs. A line of cabbages look down on the others, just like how the middle class look down on everybody while pretending to be faux peasants.

You could wait for Amoafoa in the car, but you preferred

to walk through the market. Working as a project manager at Baasiwa Art Gallery was one of the best things to have happened to you in a long time. Your boss was a kind Ghanaian American in her late fifties who thought you had great potential. It was the best-paying job you had ever had, but it wasn't just about the money. Working there also meant you had the opportunity to exhibit your work and to interact with several local artists. You were beginning to really see yourself as an artist who could thrive on his art and make a name for himself. And on your boss's prompting you planned to apply for an MFA before the end of the year. One of the things you liked about working at the gallery was that work closed at 4 p.m. (unless it was opening night for an art show or there was a special occasion) and it was fifteen minutes away from Amoafoa's office. Which meant the chances of seeing her during the weekdays were higher as compared to seeing her only during the weekends. She closed at five, and you wouldn't have minded meeting her at her office except her office was two buildings away from Tiptoe Plaza, had too many people walking through, too many vendors trying to sell you something you didn't need, not enough parking space. The two of you had settled into a routine of meeting at the old Ghana Telecoms office parking lot, which was a ten-minute drive for you and a four-minute walk for her. Some days you dozed off in the car, but most days, you liked to walk through the market. There was always something to see or hear that you could use for your art. Amoafoa knew where to find you when the car was empty.

There's an empty wooden stall to the right of the vegetable stall. A Bose PA speaker that's seen better days sits with a cord sticking out that leads to a microphone in the left hand of a skinny man with a scraggly beard, holding a green Bible in his right hand. His blue shirt is neatly tucked into his starched trousers and his sleeves are rolled all the way up. He looks ordinary, until he opens his mouth, then a deep bellowing sound gushes out like a broken pipe, and within minutes the thirsty are gathered for a sip. You imagine that's how your father was. You never met the man, unless anybody is counting his half-bloated body at his funeral. You only know him through your mother's eyes as a good-for-nothing bastard spreading his seed like an overly paid gardener. But according to your grandmother your father must have been God's mouthpiece in another life, because charm was his middle name.

A small crowd gathers around Apostle Marfo. Everybody in the market knows that Friday afternoons are for Apostle Marfo and his miracles. Every 2 p.m., he starts off with a Presbyterian hymn:

Pam hyɛ no o
pam hyɛ
Agya Noah
pam hyɛ no o
pam hyɛ no

He may look like a man created to blend in with a crowd, but the sound that comes out of his throat belongs to the low tones of a clarinet. All the market women join in, and for a few minutes, the harmonious singing feels very comforting. Apostle then gives a short sermon that doesn't last for more than fifteen minutes. He then places a brown paper bag in the middle of the stall and proceeds to crack his knuckles, in preparation for his twenty-minute countdown while he sings praises. That is what the crowd is for. That's Apostle Marfo's routine. Every Friday, he chooses three to five random people from the crowd to perform a miracle for them. It's only after the brown paper bag is full to the brim that the session starts. It's a "no coins" policy. The faster the bag fills up, the faster the miracles. You like to stand a few meters away, close enough to observe everything, far enough to not be mistaken as one of them. You always feel sorry for these religious folks. They'll slurp up everything fed to them and then judge others for not subscribing to their misery. They can keep their God all to themselves. You're happy to be faithless. Where was God when your mother was dying? Where was God when your grandmother was dying? Where was God when your supposed inheritance was taken over by all eight of your father's siblings? Where was God when Wofa Kay's promise to look after you like he would his own son expired exactly six months after your mother (his own sister) died? Where the fuck was God the countless days you went to bed without food or hope? Okay, fine, let's agree for a moment that life is much more nuanced, and struggle unequivocally grows you, but what about the countless deaths and massacres? Where exactly is God as a mother of two breaks her back selling oranges from sunup to sundown, when her profit for the week is what you spend on food and transport in a day? God is God but he no fi slap politicians when they're looting resources meant to sustain a health system that will save thousands of lives? You just couldn't reconcile a good God with a life full of trauma and strife. Unless we all collectively agreed the Christian god was a bad god. And what good is a deity so nonchalant in nature that you'd need to sweat blood to catch his attention? Ah. Christians can keep their God chale.

You step into a shaded area, disgusted and enraged about the religiosity of Ghanaians, especially the poor ones. Your watch says it's 4:50 p.m. Amoafoa will be here any moment from now. From where you're standing there's an overwhelming fetidness of armpit sweat and desperation, a mash-up of people wrinkled and relentless, tired and resigned to fate, who think their god is a juju man who throws miracles like they are treats for his well-behaved bull mastiff.

Apostle Marfo picks someone at random and tells him to make sure he never runs out of battery power, even if there's no power for days, because he will get a call that will cement his future in the next few weeks. The man who is clutching a transparent file with CURRICULUM VITAE written boldly across a sheet of paper suddenly looks hopeful. He takes his wallet out, pulls out three 10-cedi notes, and drops them into the brown paper bag. Apostle places his hand on his head, mutters a few words, and walks to the other end of the crowd.

He points at a dark-skinned girl in a yellow dress. "Whatever you're planning to do, don't do it. It will save you one day." You don't understand this whole Christianity business. Surely this man is mad, but people can't be this dim-witted. If this is how miracles work you're ready to start a business too. But yellow-dress girl is obviously stricken because she bursts into tears. Apostle places his hand on her shoulder and tries to comfort her; her back is towards you this entire time but after a while she turns and you get a good glimpse of her. The striking resemblance to Boatemaa stops you dead in your tracks. She's a busty girl with a skinny waist and glinting coal skin, and if she wasn't short you could've sworn it was Boatemaa. She moves and the crowd swallows her but the thought of Boatemaa takes hold of you the way phlegm seizes cotton. Boatemaa with her soft hands and Sunday school teacher voice. Agile multifaceted Boatemaa, who thinks the world is capable of good things. Whose mother planted a kind of fear you did not know your mind could summon when the two of you met unexpectedly at Boatemaa's apartment minutes after you and her had had sex. And how her mother had drilled you like you were answering the questionnaire that grants Christians access to the gates of heaven. Asking where you went to church, where your parents went to church, what you did, and how involved you were in church, like that had any reflection on your personhood. Boatemaa, who you had wronged way too many times for her to still be vaguely interested in you. Yes, you are appreciative of forgiveness but there's something very terrifying about a woman whose rage is quiet. It makes no sense. Shit is not supposed to be odorless. There was something very unnerving

about her unyielding want for you; there was something about
her goodness that accentuated your guilt. And you know you
should've done the decent thing and ended things with her
before starting anything with Amoafoa, but your want for
her did not run out. And yes, God or whoever could've given
Amoafoa less clanky teeth and smoother skin, and maybe a few
notches down on the clinginess. But Amoafoa has two degrees,
a well-paying job, and a Nissan Qashqai. She was born into a
family that guaranteed a transfer of generational wealth. You
couldn't both be intelligence without stilts, trying to escape the
middle class with twice as much hard work and stubborn pride.

You know you are wrong. But you are right too. Or not.
Any hard-thinking man would've picked the best bet out of the
lot. You still love Boatemaa. You love Amoafoa too. Have you
become your father? Nah, fuck that. You can never become
him. Or whatever chale. E be like that sometimes. You made
the best decision. Everybody hurts, life goes on. You haven't
even spoken to Boatemaa in months. You couldn't even if you
wanted to, seeing as she's blocked you everywhere.

"Gentleman with the cartoon shirt."

Apostle's voice interrupts your thoughts. For a long second
you don't realize he's referring to you. It's only when you notice
the people around turning to look at you that you remember
you're wearing a Simpsons T-shirt. You look up and Apostle is
pointing at you.

"Yes, you are the one I'm talking to. Abrantie, why are
you holding a grudge with a dead person? Gyae ma enka wati.
Let it go."

You skip shock and jump headfirst into fury. Your entire face is burning with anger, you're clenching hard at your jaw, everybody looks blurry, and you're breathing too hard to will your mouth to give voice to your feelings.

"Opoku," a familiar voice calls out.

You turn to see Amoafoa waving and smiling widely at you. You're suddenly so relieved to see her. You have never been this happy for her to show up. You turn back to look at Apostle with what you hope is a deadly look, and then you start walking towards Amoafoa.

Toxic male partner

This recipe is handed down from a father even though the son swears he's nothing like him

Ingredients

A father's 3rd or 6th child (a father's 1st child in his late teens works too)
Has 5–12 siblings or none at all
¼ tsp. self-awareness
2 cups (280g) ego
5 ¼ cups (1000g) hypersexuality
Identifies as an egalitarian in his twenties, then as a feminist 2 years later then as an ally 3 years later
Hates "labeling" relationships with women because it's too stifling

Preparation

First, have a difficult childhood

eating sorrow for breakfast

VICTORIA

Three days after I'm dead, Mama grips the knob of the bed-post to steady her weak knees. She's sitting on my bed folding the bright blue towel I bought from Shoprite. They were pricy enough to assume good quality, but my nipples would trap bits of fluff after bathing so I used coconut oil to get them off. My black bra with the butterfly lace netting is on the floor beside her feet. I loved that bra because it boosted my boobs ever so slightly without giving them an illusion of ampleness.

In all the twenty-eight years, three months, and six days I spent alive, not once did I see my mother cry. Unless we're counting the day she teared up from rage over an okada driver for ramming into the front of her car and damaging her bumper. Mary Otu crying? Rarest shit in all of Adenta.

My mother is a woman who doesn't poke at a wound to test for its soreness. I know this because a few days after her only brother died, she gave all his clothes away and kept only the pictures of him as a boy, smiling with two missing front teeth. Seeing her in my room chanting "mothers are not supposed to bury daughters," her tiny frame bent over, folding and unfolding my clean clothes, and cleaning my shoes like I was going to show up any second, wasn't something I expected. People used to think she was my younger sister anytime they saw the two of us together because even though I had inherited her piercing brown eyes, lack of eyebrows, and lips like someone tipped a bottle top too enthusiastically in a counters game, I was bigger than her and almost two inches taller.

One Friday afternoon when I was nine years old, she smacked my head on the side of the secondhand fridge in the hallway after I told her I wasn't going to wash my father's socks because he wouldn't pay my school fees. I dropped the alasa I had just washed.

"He is still the head of this family. Just because I pay your school fees, Victoria, doesn't mean you can disrespect your father. Foolish girl!"

I pinned my eyes to the blood orange half-fist fruit on the blue linoleum floor.

All our lives we were forced to be audience to an eternal rant; my father's failed entrepreneurial attempts at the risk of her savings, his waning interest in his own children after they were past toddlerhood, his lack of support for her dreams and failures while demanding a participating audience for his, the heavy flirtations. But none of these were as unbearable for my mother as his care for his other child. Three weeks after I was born, as hard as my father tried to hide it, my mother found out that he had fathered another child with another woman. She was born nine days before I was born; she was born on my father's birthday. And my father had the genius idea to name both of us after his mother. Victoria Otu. So not only did my mother have to find out there was another child, but that her child now shared a name, a name she felt belonged to her daughter and her daughter alone. But the truly worst part, as the years rolled by, wasn't that there had been another woman—my father swore it was a mistake, he never sought to wound her, and my mother was his one and only soul mate—it was that it was clear as day that he loved this other Victoria more than he loved her children. And despite her despair, she continued to love him.

She confused me, my mother. She would complain about my father to my brother and me, and then get offended by our animosity towards him.

I did not want my father at my graduation. Frankly, he wasn't particularly enthusiastic about being there either. So I skipped inviting him. But my mother fought me like the survival of our already dysfunctional family depended on him being present at the graduation, and she slapped me harder than I'd ever been slapped when I told her the only thing that made him my father was his contribution to fertilizing her eggs.

The look in her eyes before she hit me, as though she was greatly pained doing this but had started already, so had to finish. How her hand arrived with a resounding clap into my skin before the dizzying whir danced around my head.

The sound of her hand landing on my cheek echoed in my ears. Days later, I described it on the phone to Selorm as bad sex.

"What do you mean it was like bad sex?"

"Like the sex has already started, but instead of pleasure you're being pummeled like meat."

"I see."

"Yeah. She kept hitting me and crying at the same time, as if she was convincing herself she had to—"

"Um, not to cut you but—when you say bad sex, you don't mean bad sex with me. Right?"

"What the hell? It was just an example. I'm trying to make you understand what has become of my mother and me. What has this got anything to do with us?"

"Yeah, I know, I just think . . . you don't just use an analogy like that if you haven't experienced it. We're close enough for you to tell me if anything between us wasn't—"

"This has absolutely nothing to do with us."

"Okay, yeah, that's good to know. But like, why did you use that analogy?"

"Why not?"

"Okay, so when did we . . . um, you have bad sex?"

"Are you serious? So fuck my trauma with my mum. Let's forget about all that and discuss bad sex because I used that phrase?"

"That's not what I meant, Vicky. I'm just saying."

I hung up. Even in the middle of a woman's sorrow, a man wants your existence to revolve around him.

If you want to cast my father's nonchalance for his family

and his love for his other child in a broader light, it would be akin to the unfettered love Ghanaians who live abroad have for Accra when they're visiting during their summer break. How they praise roadside waakye like it is the best food to ever exist. How they prefer to roll the car windows down instead of putting on the AC in 33-degree weather because "the fresh air is full of flavor." How they parade the Ghana flag in every single bio from LinkedIn to Twitter.

My father made his other child worthy of worship, and relegated us to nonchalance. He didn't attempt to hide his indifference or make an effort with us. There were no crumbs of love to eat up. He created a rift between us, and I held it apart.

I treated my father with silence. He met me with unfinished sentences and wordless grunts that evolved into even longer silences. I didn't entirely know how fathers were supposed to be but I was sure they weren't supposed to be like this. He probably would've been a better father if he were absent. I was certain the other Victoria thought the world of him. I would too, if I only saw my father a few times a year and received gifts throughout the year to compensate for his absence. My attitude towards him was fueled by stupid hope that he would somehow care for my personhood. Take a genuine interest in me. Ask me how my day was going or why I had gained six pounds. Buy me a birthday card, or surprise me with a new phone. For the longest time I wanted my father to be a father. The year I turned twenty-six was the year he turned fifty-two. It was exactly a year after my graduation. On my mother's insistence I planned a daddy-daughter dinner at a restaurant I had found online that dished out food in animal shapes. We laughed about the food, I got him customized cuff links, and he even got me a funny birthday card from Yobbings; I was surprised he even knew about them. It was going well—that is, until I asked him if he was or had ever been depressed. The thought had seized hold of me weeks before; it was the only explanation I could think of that made sense for my father's attitude towards his family. The blatant disinterest, his complete withdrawals, his seeming forgetfulness, the detachment, the long silences. I knew he was not of a generation that believed depression a thing for black people but I just needed a reason to latch on to. I even told him I was asking because I had depressive episodes too.

If I had stood in the middle of the neighborhood with a megaphone and called my father names it would have caused only slightly less of an annoyance. I had never seen him this angry. He called me disrespectful, crazy, spoiled. Said he had given me too much liberty, because how else would I feel confident to ask him this. Dinner ended abruptly and we sat in silence on the way back home. How foolish of me to think I could talk to my father, to ask to be shown who he was and to be seen by him as a person and not a by-product of his marriage, a burdening responsibility.

It was my last attempt. I adopted his apathy and learned to live with it. And we would've continued with our lives if my mother just let things be. Our animosity made her itch and she was determined to change it. She sent me on errands for him, sat me next to him at the dining table. Made me cook for him, pushing for dialogue, anything to fill the silence. And when it

yielded more silence, a quiet anger would descend on her. It
was as if she was convinced she had hacked her way through
living with my father and raising us, and if she could do it,
why couldn't I? We spent a year perfecting how to be strangers living together. Months later, she found out the money she
lent my father was start-up capital for his other daughter—
continued penance for his long absences in her life. After she
threw a coat hanger at me for telling her she allowed my father
to disrespect her, I flirted with nonexistence. I thought hard of
how peaceful it would be to not be here. To not have to wake
up, go to work, see my mother, engage with people, worry
about getting through every single day without buckling underneath this weight of darkness. I thought hard about dying
and how quickly I could speed it up. I sat on my bed holding an
ice cube against the welt on my forehead, and then I packed a
few clothes in a bag and left home for my best friend's house.
I knew I couldn't stay there for long; she shared a room with
two siblings. But going back home seemed unthinkable.

On the way to Ayeley's, I tried to cling to the idea of
belonging to a family that was full of tenderness and love.
A family that you had good things to say about when a TV
presenter randomly stopped you in the middle of the street for
a Mother's Day campaign show. Where you said "I love you"
to each other and being around them didn't fill you with angst.

Ayeley took my bag from me and made me lie down
without asking questions. She knew I liked kelewele so she
made some for me. In a tone between anger and pain, I told
her every detail. She listened without interrupting. As I was

speaking, I realized how absurd the entire thing was and burst into tears. She looked at me uneasily and left the room, returning with a tissue and a hug after I had blown my nose.

"You must think I'm spoiled," I told her, holding the used tissue.

"Don't be silly, you have every right to be upset, this is not okay, Vic. Your mother threw a coat hanger at you! A coat hanger! You're better than me. I would've thrown three shoes back at her."

In spite of myself, I laugh.

"I'm sorry all of this is happening. I don't know what to say about your father. I know you guys were having issues but I didn't know it was this bad. You can stay as long as you need."

It was settled; I would spend my days here, and sleep in her aunty Jasmine's salon in the evenings until I figured things out. Her parents were strict, but she had asserted her stubbornness early as a teenager, and could get away with things you wouldn't expect a pastor's child to get away with.

Staying with Ayeley wasn't all bad but I didn't know how good a mattress I had until I left home. I missed my bed. I missed my pillow. I missed the smell of the detergent my mother used for laundry. I missed the luxury of having the kitchen to myself. I missed hearing my mother complain about my brother spending all his time playing video games. I missed my mother's cooking. I even missed treating my father to silence. But both my mother and I held on to stubbornness. So I slept on the hard linoleum floor of the hair salon. My brother called every day asking me to come back home, but after two weeks, he stopped asking and called only to check in and update me. I had stopped waiting for my mother to call me. The first night I didn't return home, I stayed up all night waiting for her to call. I was angry, but clearly, so was she.

Selorm's emotions overwhelmed me. He went from feeling anger at my parents for creating an environment so toxic I felt the need to leave home, to feeling guilt about not having his own place so I could be more comfortable. No matter how many times I tried to convince him he was being extremely helpful with the weekly cash he was giving me, he still felt burdened by his not enoughness.

Ayeley and I left the house in the mornings, she to work, and me to job search. Some weekends she had friends over and we cooked for them, and I spent Sundays with Selorm at his house.

In the beginning, I was confident I could find a job with my sociology degree, save up enough money in a few months to rent a place, and have time to focus on my career and my relationship with Selorm. We had talked vaguely about marriage before I left home. We both didn't want kids, but we thought a small wedding and a small apartment a little farther away from the city would suit us. After three months of not finding a job, I was desperate and depressed. I had sent CVs to more than fifty companies. I had even walked into places and offered to work for free for the first month. I was tired. On my twenty-eighth birthday I woke up to a rejection email for a job I enjoyed interviewing for and was almost certain I would get. I lay down and cried. A cry that started as a soft sob and progressed into a deep stuttering howl that shook my body violently. I was unable to will my body to get out of bed, too crushed by the obligation to stay alive to make an effort, bearing the weight of what it meant to have nowhere to place my tiredness, marked by the passing of time.

Ayeley tried to help. She swore a makeover would make me feel better, so that Saturday during the day, we went over to her aunt Jasmine's to fix a frontal weave.

"Are you also twenty-seven? I hope you have a boyfriend o . . . oh, you're even twenty-eight, when are you bringing him home? What does he do? Me, I like tall black men o, so that we can have nice babies. Oh. What do you mean you will not have children? Stop that, you will have two children. Only two. I hope you're not also doing feminism like Ayeley, men don't like pitripitri women o."

Ayeley apologized for her aunty's remarks. I swore I didn't care about these old women who knew their husbands were sleeping with everything in skirts but still had the energy to shame young women for being single or not wanting kids. We laughed about it later but I stayed up all night because I couldn't get *twenty-eight and unmarried* out of my head. It's not like I wanted to get married right away, but suddenly the realization of turning twenty-eight with nothing to call my own made everything feel worse. When I finally managed to fall asleep, I had a terrible dream. I was in the middle of a street wearing nothing but black linen panties with silver bells hanging at the edges. All the Ghanaian aunties and creepy Ghanaian men were singing *sha-sha-sha-shaaaame* like their lives depended on it, and I was bawling like someone had sworn to cut my head off. It was a dream that would repeat itself for a number of days. When I told Ayeley she laughed and told me I was watching too much *Game of Thrones*.

I kept waiting for my mother to ask me to come back home. I broke down on the phone one day with Deanna and told her everything. Told her that I was in a state of suspension. Even though I had a home, I was homeless, jobless, broke, and righteously proud. I had a father, but he might as well be dead. I loved my mother, but I did not really like her. And when I was done sniffing my way through talking, she said to me, *Let me know if there's anything I can do to help*. As if I didn't just spill my entire guts to her; what more did she want to know before she deduced she could help?

After eight and a half months, I found a job as a PA for a lawyer and moved back home, only because it was a ten-minute drive from home and I found out my father had left the house. I was hopeful his absence would ease the tension between my mother and me. But she was considerably worse, perpetually irritable, deeply angry and sad, and often abusive.

Because my boss knew I lived close to the office, work hours stretched to 7 p.m., sometimes 8. But on this day he had to fly out of the country for a meeting, so I was home by 4:30. I had bought ginger biscuits and a small bowl of Fanice on the way, planning to spend the rest of my day watching movies and stuffing my face with junk food. But just before I could settle into a movie, Selorm called. He was reserving a table for us at a fancy restaurant, and I had an hour and a half to dress up for a dinner date. I couldn't remember when last we did something like this. I was excited. I spent forty minutes trying on different outfits and finally settled on a beige corset maxi dress that I bought a year ago but hadn't had the opportunity to wear yet. I was looking for my wine lipstick when my mother's voice interrupted my flow.

"Is that the dress you're wearing?" She was leaning hard on the door handle.

"Yes."

"Maybe wear another one? This one is not working."

"What do you mean this one is not working?"

"It's just not working, can't you see in the mirror, your tummy is in several folds. Don't you have a dress that has a flare to it or something? Something nice?"

"No, I like how I'm looking, thank you."

"Ahh, okay o, don't say I didn't look out for you."

"You never have anything nice to say."

"Oh. Is that what I get for trying to help you pick a good outfit?"

"Yeah, you're not helping."

"Well, if you insist on wearing this at least suck your tummy in a little."

"Why do you always do this? I'm wearing a corset dress and yet somehow this is not enough for you? What do you want from me? This is how my body is, this is how I am built!"

"Erm, okay. First of all, I was just trying to help, feel free to not take my advice, it's not like you listen to me anyway. Secondly, this is not how you are 'built,' young lady, you ate yourself into this body. Nobody in this family is built like this."

She turned to leave, closing the door a little too hard on her way. I stood there, all desire to step out in a dress that a few minutes ago I was in love with drained out of me.

At the mercy of my mother's "helpful" words and her mood swings, I was agitated all the time. My brother was barely home; he was dating a girl whose father had gifted her an apartment at Cantonments, so he spent most of his time with her. I felt alone. I was alone.

Our collective sadness stank up the house. It got into everything, into my clothes, how they hung loose on my body like they didn't belong. It got into my food, everything tasted like old coins, eating was an act I engaged in to merely stay alive. It got into my body, how anxiety scraped the lining of my stomach. It got into my relationships: I quarreled with Selorm, called him names, hurled nefarious words at him, had screaming contests with my mother at least twice a week.

Work offered little to no escape. Unhappiness descended from a hierarchy of casual dissatisfaction to a kind of moroseness, slipping comfortably into a normalized task of my day to day, and finally to a state of nothingness. So the decision to leave my body wasn't a hard one. I just needed time to be still. Even if for a while.

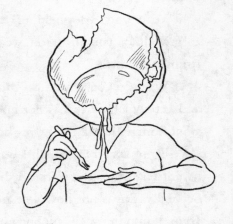

footnote

BAABA

It happened in your twenty-fifth year, the year you enrolled in a five-month programming class because there were too many hours in your afternoons and you needed something to do with your hands. Your sister, Naana, had been having cramps so severe they had paralyzed her left leg. Three years, several hospitals, and yet there wasn't a proper diagnosis. She would hear of a doctor, visit a hospital with high hopes, spend precious money on different tests, and come back home with nothing but more painkillers. The pain got so bad that on some days she needed assistance to bathe, so being the loving sister that you were, you had volunteered to stay home and take care of her. Her afternoon pills usually knocked her out for at least four hours, so you enrolled yourself in a two-hour C++ class that was fifteen minutes away from the house. Paa Kwesi was one of the tutors.

He was good with the students because he had a way of deconstructing the most complex problems into simple steps without making you feel like an idiot. He had a thick afro and a small tuft of beard sitting on his chin, and his glasses masked his half-closed eyes. On the first day of class "Mr. Robertson" was spelled out on the white board, but everybody called him "Sir."

You struggled with the course; it didn't help much that you were the oldest in the class. Most of the students were high school graduates waiting to start university, and here was a university graduate struggling to keep up. You were ready to quit, but Mr. Robertson offered to spend twenty extra minutes with you after class, and if you didn't see any difference in two weeks, you were free to quit. True to his word, by the end of that week you didn't feel completely clueless, and by week two, you were helping another girl with her code. In the fourth week he asked you to call him Paa Kwesi. Three months after being in the class he asked you out on a movie date. Before the movie started you were so nervous you weren't sure you would actually pay attention, but you discover it's a horror-adjacent movie and you become so invested you don't notice immediately that he's been staring at you for a while now. His eyes meet yours and you smile.

"I just realized something," he whispers a little too aggressively. "In this very moment, I am the happiest I have ever been, because I get to spend time with the hottest girl alive."

And just like that, you feel a familiar wetness in your linen panties. So when he asks you weeks later if you would be his girlfriend, of course you say yes.

You take showers together, his shirts look good on you.

You have breakfast in bed and spend Saturdays analyzing crime movies like the two of you are being paid for it. The way he holds your bag in public makes you believe in forever and you're surprised by how good his kontomire stew is.

Your cousin moves in to help take care of Naana, who has finally been correctly diagnosed with endometriosis and has started a new treatment that seems to be helping. You see an advertisement on Twitter for a bank job and apply for it. After two interviews, you get the job. You're happy; new job, new boyfriend, new treatment for Naana. Your life couldn't get any better.

The first time, you see a text message on his phone from a "beans seller" asking if he enjoyed the head this time around, he denies it profusely and gets mad at you for insinuating that he would ever cheat.

The second time, you see red underwear a size bigger than yours at his place, he denies any knowledge of it, you don't speak for days, until he convinces you that he finally knows how it got there. His friend Joojo and his girlfriend were in his apartment for a day and must have left it. He even has Joojo call you to tell you as testament to this, describing the panties in detail.

A month later your phone dies before you could tell Paa you're coming over, which is why you catch him with another girl.

You'd been dating for just eight months. You weren't going to die because he was a cheating bastard.

Lies.

It hurt like a motherfucker. You cried so much it surprised even you. You would be perfectly fine, working and processing a client's request, and then out of nowhere stupid tears would ambush you. You cried so much you were freshening up your makeup three times a day just so you looked less like a bruised tomato.

Naana said you would be fine in a month, and anyway, you didn't want to have a kid whose nose looked like it would fall off any minute. You would've believed her if Paa would just stop calling. You had blocked him everywhere, but that didn't stop him. He called and pleaded and parked in front of your house at odd hours. After coming home to see a hand-written note begging to see you just one last time so he could explain things, you gave in. A part of you needed to know why, as if that information would magically restore your feelings to default settings, but you needed to know. So you agreed to meet at his place after work the next Friday.

You wait ten minutes to ring the bell. Paa takes your hand and you follow quietly like a lost creature. He kneels beside you on the bed, buries his face in your lap, and starts sobbing. After what feels like forever he starts shuffling sentences out of his mouth.

She doesn't mean anything to me. I am so sorry. I didn't mean to hurt you. I love you very much. I haven't slept in weeks because I can't stop thinking about you. I need you back in my life. I'm really really sorry, Baaba.

It is as if someone suddenly splashed wet poo on your arm, like something heavy is trying to suffocate you and you just can't wait to leave the room. He is kneeling with his arms wrapped around your waist, you tell him you can't do this anymore, and you try to take his hands off you but his grip tightens. You call him a liar and a cheating bastard, and it feels good to say it out loud. He tells you that you can call him anything as long as you stay, to which you spit out "NEVER" with such ferocity it must have broken something in him, because suddenly he pushes you onto the bed and tries to take your sandals off. You are angry enough, you stamp his chest with your left leg, and it fuels him more because he presses his knees into your legs, trapping you and holding both of your wrists so you stop slapping him with such force. Your wrists are burning. He chants "You're mine" over and over, and you are crying and begging and cursing. He unzips his shorts and pries your thighs open, and you fight even harder but it doesn't last, because his knees are pressing into yours and the pain is so intense you can think of nothing else but the pain, you can barely move. So when you feel him pushing his way inside you, the fight is gone out of you, you only want it to be over. Thank whoever is listening because in a few minutes he spasms and collapses on top of you, and whispers "I love you, Baaba" in your ear. This time when you try to leave he doesn't stop you. You put your sandals on and walk out of the house.

You walk for several minutes instead of taking a cab home. You walk as if you want to outwalk your body and leave it behind. To this day, you still don't know how you got home, or what happened between the time you left and the morning after. You only know your defeated body underneath his, the hurried sound of his breath as he pinned you down, and light leaving your eyes when you could no longer fight back. You start to shrink, not immediately, but it begins.

Two years ago my whole body swallowed the shape of a footnote. It isn't visible, of course, my skin is still a mound of flesh that Aba, the woman in the cubicle next to me, pokes at with her manicured fingers whenever it is lunchtime. I speak all the time, it isn't something I can avoid, working in a bank and all. But when I speak I sound like an echo, like I have gone and crouched in the darkest, snuggest part of my body, and another me is speaking five layers above me while I cheer her on with sad eyes.

Nothing much has changed. I am still a teller at LeapBank. My makeup is flawless and my red lipstick still looks like it's God-ordained. Serving customers all day with a gentle smile, I cash checks, receive deposits and record transactions. My course mate from university doesn't understand why I'm still a teller, tells me that with my degree in Business Administration I should be one of the managers working in the back office. She's right, but I like the opportunity to engage with people. For the first time in my life, I am grateful for work. Grateful for the hours it demands of me. It takes me three hours to wake up and take a shower and get dressed and make it through traffic to be at work by 8 a.m. The earliest I leave is 7 p.m., getting home by 9, worn out enough to pass out, ready for the alarm to wake me up at 5 to start the routine all over.

Nobody at work knows what happened. Not even my big sister, Naana, even though we live in the same house. People can't tell I'm probably living in another dimension, that my body might be here but everything else is an echo away. I don't expect them to. These things don't exactly spurt out as gas from the orifices of your body. There's a madwoman who sits on the ground a few steps away from the beans seller down the street. The teller in the cubicle next to me said a borla car knocked her son over on a Friday while picking up trash from the houses in the neighborhood, and the mortuary gave his corpse to the hospital's medical school because she couldn't pay the bill. So every Friday you'll find her at the medical school, hurling curses so full of venom that even unbelievers will call on an unknown power for protection.

I feel like a donated corpse, except nobody's hurling curses in my name. I wonder how long a body can sustain life before it starts to decay.

Twenty-seven going on sixty-seven. I don't know how to think of it without drowning, I don't know how to speak of it without fear of being blamed. I want to tell John, he's the closest thing to a brother I've ever known, but a peculiar mash of fear and pain keeps me quiet, so when I call him in the middle of the night trying to live through yet another panic attack, he stays awake with me on the phone, reads poems out loud, narrates Nollywood movies until I fall asleep. I lose count of the number of times I want to tell Naana.

Two years ago my body swallowed the shape of a footnote. And I sincerely thought I would never step away from the background. I thought I could never live boldly like I belonged to the main stage. I thought I could never smile at another man, lie next to another man, even have a normal conversation with another man.

But then I met Koku, who worked with autistic kids while completing a masters in banking and finance, and whose best friend's cousin's girlfriend taught at the same programming school Paa taught at. Koku, who thought my navel was the most mesmerizing thing ever. Who would stay up late and wait till he got an "I'm home" text from me before he allowed himself to fall asleep. With whom I could have three-hour phone conversations without realizing that much time had passed by. And when I felt safe enough to ponder over what had happened, it was him I opened up to.

"Babs, I'm so mad and sorry this happened. I'm so disgusted. I wish you had reported him to the police right away."

"Lol. And say what, Koku? Where would I even start? How would I explain that my ex-boyfriend had raped me? Was it even rape? It's not as if we hadn't had sex before . . ."

"Of course it was rape! How is that not rape? I am ready to fight anybody who does not think that is rape."

"We both know the systems here are near useless. The police will ask me, 'Why didn't you scream or fight?' Or 'What were you doing there in the first place if you'd broken up?' I'm trying to remember, but I'm not even sure at that moment I had the money needed to get a doctor's report for the police."

"My God. Men are bastards."

Koku understood. He held me like I was a golden egg and made me soft. Gave me room to be soft and doubtful and weak and whole again.

Two weeks later during a football match between Barcelona and Real Madrid, Paa Kwesi tweeted commentary on Neymar's prowess, and tagged three guys, including Koku, in his tweet. And Koku replied, like it was a fucking water cooler conversation he *had* to participate in.

I was sitting on the living room floor with a jar of groundnut paste in front of me, eating banana dipped in groundnut paste when I saw the tweet. I felt my throat squeezed tight by a sharp betrayal. I could hear my chest pounding in my ears. There was a tiny voice inside my head telling me it was just a tweet, just a reply, just a string of words. But a louder and determined voice drowned it out with conviction. I put the groundnut paste away and went straight to bed. I wanted to call Koku right away, but I didn't even know where I would start, how I could possibly explain this pain. So instead I lay there staring at the tweet, dazed by its existence, at how a random sentence could poison my happiness in an instant. Finally, I gave in to overthinking and started to cry. I cried until I fell asleep.

But I slept badly. It was still dark outside when I woke up and I had a bad headache. I tapped the right side of the bed until I found my phone. I had fallen asleep staring at the tweet and it was the first thing I saw when I opened the phone.

My healing was spoiled. Indelibly marked by this small betrayal. The more I tried to convince myself that this was

too small a thing to be worked up about, the more it deep-
ened the heartbreak. It was as if because I trusted Koku with
my vulnerability, that trust had magnified this small betrayal.
Made it seem bigger and much closer than it appeared.

I know I should give myself time before I reach out, but I
open the message app and start typing.

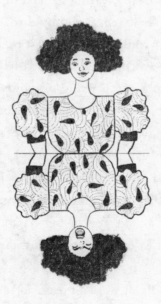

re: how are you and i miss you

DEANNA

From: Deanna Asante <deannawails@email.com>
Sent: Saturday, January 19, 2019 10:42 AM
To: Yaa Amoafoa Ankonam <yaamako@email.com>
Subject: Re: how are you and I miss you

    I am sorry it has taken me this long to reply to your email. These days, my life feels like a life-sized painting I have to finish at a hurried pace; not because I want to, but because I have missed all my deadlines. I am busy mostly; working, traveling, raising kids, not writing. Which annoys me. I want to write, or rather, I want to have written. But there isn't enough time to save some for writing, and when there is enough time, there isn't any inspiration. But in all, I am well, I guess. Nhyira started crawling last Tuesday. I didn't realize it was possible to be so proud of someone for crawling between two sofas. Yao and I felt like the proud parents of a Grammy Award winner!

I know I am going to sound like one of those adults who swear life after school is more stressful and complicated but I really wish you would worry less about school and try to enjoy yourself. In less than a year you'll be done with your masters and working full-time, and commence with marriage and kids—full-mode adulting. And trust me that shit is ten times more debilitating then you can ever imagine. Because when you're trying to meet a deadline, you will realize the strong smell hitting you is a combination of baby shit from under the dining table, and burnt fried plantain that you had been looking forward to eating because of a one-week kelewele craving that wouldn't stop taunting you, and there will be no one to direct your anger to, and you will want to cry, but there will be no time for tears. Do you know how frustrating that is? To want to cry but there simply is no time to? I'm not sure I'm doing this adulting thing well. Or is this what adulting is? Putting your misery on hold because there's shit to do? 😕

I am trying to live life one day at a time. It's been nine weeks since they found Vicky's lifeless body in her house. That she killed herself is an unspoken truth that has been carefully tucked away. As far as everybody else knows, she died after a brief illness. I can't believe I was expected to go for her funeral. Whatever for? To see a display of her body in its lifelessness? I don't want to see a dead version of her. I don't want my last visual memory of her to be of her in a coffin. I haven't even fully come to terms with her being dead.

I understand depression in the abstract, but I can't make

sense of it when it presents itself in front of me. I think I even know what it means to be depressed, I know what it means to want to put life on hold, if even for a moment. I know what it means to have no desire to persist, what it means to want to die. And I know depression is a feeling and feelings aren't monolithic no matter how similar they can be—but to go ahead and drain the living out of you, I cannot understand it, Amoafoa. I am struggling to accept that Vicky had a darkness that stalked her relentlessly to the point of destruction. I know she's been having some issues for a while now, but this—this is a lot. I have turned this over and over in my head and each time I feel a barrage of emotions rummaging itself in my chest: unhappiness, anguish, rage—I have been reduced to a woman who has spiteful conversations with a dead girl for being so overwhelmed with her suffering that she took her life. I feel both anger and sorrow. It is hard to come to terms with this finality. So I will not hear her voice again? She will not saunter into a room and fill the place with her deep laughter? My God.

There has to be an easier way to wring out grief.

Prof. Gariba hugs you every time you ace his tests? Sounds like you're going to get lots of hugs this semester. He sounds a little overenthusiastic though, but I'm glad someone is celebrating your genius in little doses. When next I see you we will forget I am a thirty-two-year-old with two kids and stay up all night talking about life and boys. (I just remembered that darkskinned boy we were crushing on for weeks because he would tweet endlessly about books and politics and feminism, and how we had to block him because he "wasn't going to instantly believe XO was a rapist just because six girls said so." Waste of crush! <insert eye roll emoji>)

You know how I am always praising this university for its diversity and inclusiveness? Well, that's canceled! Canceled! You hear me? I have finally been given a reason to bite my tongue, which is such a shame, I had carved for myself a safe space in this place, and for this to happen feels like being robbed in broad daylight. We were having a departmental meeting in the Rawlings Building when Nhyira woke up and lunged right into tears. She is normally with my mother but the woman had fallen on her bad knee and so I didn't want to trouble her, besides it was a holiday, the meeting was to last for not more than two hours. The only reason this meeting was happening on a holiday was because there had been an ongoing debate for weeks in one of the second-year classes that had reached faculty, about how national issues and academia ought to be fused with pop culture if there was any hope of truly impacting the masses.

Nhyira had been feeding for over twenty minutes now and was so quiet I thought she had fallen asleep. I was in the middle of telling Prof. Fianko about how some aspects of academia had to be repackaged in the different forms of pop culture, and by doing that we could move knowledge from the classroom to the streets—and make knowledge easily accessible. I was too distracted to notice that Nhyira had detached her mouth from my nipple and was staring at God-knows-what. Of course I didn't realize that my swollen left breast was exposed, and I probably wouldn't have until after the class if Mr. Oko with his dirty skin hadn't snarled at me for being indecent in an academic space. Can you imagine? Fucking pervert told me I was being indecent in an academic space. As if the school exists in a different universe and not Ghana, where women breastfeed everywhere! I felt SO embarrassed and exposed. I was too stunned to say a word, everybody else was quiet for what felt like an hour. It was Mrs. Antoa who mockingly asked him if there were no breastfeeding mothers in his hometown. The room was instantly flooded with giggles as though they were farts that had been held in for too long.

I was too upset to stay and left the building right away. I am sure they asked him to send a handwritten apology to me, because I found a note on my desk the next day, but I cannot get that moment out of my head. His audacity and entitlement over the space so much that he felt inclined to dictate how I should inhabit it, the uncomfortable silence of everybody in that room—I can't help feeling like someone who was groped without her permission.

Enough about my messy complicated life. I read your email so many times Yao asked me if I was learning for an exam. I miss you.

I have been thinking about your question. "Is love in totality possible? Pure, unblemished, not harmful, progressive, absolute love?" It's both frustrating and freeing that love is a shapeless formless thing. My immediate answer is, of course, no. But I also want to say that I do not really know the answer to this question.

I think you mean to ask if the theory of absolutism can exist in love. Absolutism in this context is the belief that one can or should love completely to the benefit of the loved—there can't be any pain, or suffering or hurt—it should be love in all its glorious goodness. If we claim love is the greatest thing on earth, then it should be the one thing that should be all good. Absolutism here could mean, for example, that Idi Amin should only be seen as an evil selfish leader who slaughtered his people like chickens. It makes no room for him to be a good lover too, someone who was affectionate and yearned for another's touch, someone who perhaps saved his money so he could buy a new cloth for his lover, not because he wants to be hailed as selfless, but merely to see her smile. Absolutism wants us to believe that because Mother Teresa is largely known for her kind heart, she never harbored dislike or irritation, or held grudges, or had tantrums, or never thought of masturbation. Or that by virtue of being great at adoration in relationships, it crosses out my inconsistency in being present or showing up. Absolutism doesn't make room for nuances: it is a single story that everyone is glued to, and likes, as a matter of fact. But just because we like something as we see it doesn't mean that is all there is to it.

I feel like I am already going nowhere with this, not just a vague nothingness, but a certain specific point within the nothingness. What I mean is that I may be going nowhere, but in going nowhere, I hope I arrive somewhere.

Let me see if I can explain this in another way. Absolutism is like when a new mother says, "Having a child has expanded my capacity for love more than I could ever imagine." And that is sweet and true, but is that all there is to having a child? How did she respond to her body yielding open to make space for another human being? Was birthing ridiculous? Did it feel like menstrual cramps, only this time the pain was raised to the power of 25? With your muscles twisting themselves within you? Did she curse and bite her own lip and scream and beg for it to stop? Did she let out a loud fart or a gooey mess and not even have the time or self-awareness to care? Love includes all these details. Love is messy and nitpicky and complicated. Absolutism doesn't purport to be.

I love you, Amoafoa, the thought of you is like a switch I inadvertently reach for. But do I check up on you all the time? I don't. Is it because I am busy most of the time? I AM busy most of the time. But sometimes I am not. Sometimes I am too tired. Sometimes I am free but I don't feel like it. Sometimes I want to be alone, sometimes I forget. Does that mean I love you any less?

So to answer your question, is absolute love possible? I don't think so. But love can be good. Love is good. In all its messiness, love is supposed to be good.

Are you asking this because of Opoku? Is he loving you like he cannot unglue his existence from yours? What do you mean by you fear you cannot live without his body or voice or intellect? Why is there a premise for this thought? And what does "I love him more than my mind can allow, despite his jittery feet" mean? What does jittery feet mean here? Do I need to write a scathing

email that will drag his entire ancestry? Do I need to start sum-
moning my ancestors?

I hope you're eating well and not plucking your eyebrows in
an attempt to blot out anxiety. I'm sending you six voice notes:

- snippets of me giggling over Nyhira singing or blab-
  bering or whatever sound babies make after they've
  had their fill
- excerpts from this brilliant Nigerian IfeOluwa Nihinlola's
  debut novel
- a failed attempt at ASMR with M&Ms because I couldn't
  stop laughing (also here's a link of this black woman
  eating cabbages so ridiculously I laughed until I cried,
  https://blkwmneatingcabbage)
- commentary on a Nollywood movie (I watched a Nollywood movie for YOU!)
- me laughing so hard at a monologue in a Kumawood
  movie (because I really need you to fall in love with
  Lil Win too, I can't be the only one infected with Yao's
  obsession), and
- a poem I wrote for you.

See you soon, eat well for me.

    Love,
    D.

Dear Auntie Adisa...

Dear Auntie Adisa,

I'm a 27-year-old male in a serious relationship with a 25-year-old lady. I love my girlfriend, she is a smart woman (top of her class), attentive to my needs, does a lot of things for me—she cooks for me and cleans regularly, even stocks my fridge sometimes without me asking. My only problem is that I don't like her friends very much. She has three friends—the oldest is 30—who sometimes poison her with negative thoughts and cause her to question my authority. I am very sure it is because of her friends, she wasn't like this when we started dating, what do you think I should do? Can I tell her to keep some distance from her friends without sounding bad?
Disturbed man—Takyiman.

Dear Disturbed man,

Platonic relationships are very important for every individual. I am sure you have your own friends who you occasionally hang out with. Your girlfriend sounds like a nice young lady who cares very much for you. Attempting to isolate her from her friends doesn't sound like a very bright idea to me—it can result in resentment should her friends abandon her. It will however be a great advantage to you if you made an effort to get to know her friends too —you don't necessarily have to be their friends too—but you can be involved in their interests via them interacting with your girlfriend—this way they can potentially be your friends too and advise her in your best interest.
—Auntie Adisa

politicians all demma mordas

MAAYAA

SECTION A
[50 marks]

In very simple and clear terms establish a marker(s) for your national identity. Distinctly illustrate what makes your city stand out.

*You are advised to spend about **six months** on this section.*

If God's love for a country is measured by the number of beautiful women it has, Maayaa's beauty alone would count for 10 percent of that number. Her waist is a dream. Her breasts are a hundred manifestos. Her skin is an edible vintage pendant necklace on a chocolate cake. If God had an answering machine it would belch her voice. Her ambition is the stuff national budgets are made of. All that, and for what?

No amount of beauty and street smartness was changing the

grim reality that she was a young woman in her mid-twenties living in a country with the PR of peacock feathers and the functionality of a crippled farm chicken. Ghana was aging her. The rate at which dumsor threw her into a deep depression surprised even her. How the entire country was being forced to adjust to rolled-out blackouts was beyond her. To have twelve-hour blackouts every other day meant that twenty-four hours out of the forty-hour week were unproductive. There's very little you can do in a city that is heavily reliant on electricity. Her mother's cold-store business didn't survive the first quarter of the year. Not only was she not making any profit but she was losing her capital and running into debt. After two weeks, everything in the big freezer had gone bad; you couldn't even feed it to street dogs (unless you wanted to poison them). By March, the "Maa Lydia's Cold Store" blue lettering on the white corrugated plastic sign that made the twenty-foot container store a cold store was taken down. Maayaa felt particularly frustrated by dumsor because she worked for a small printing press in Newtown. The company had a generator but they could not afford to fuel it for twelve hours three times a week. So they asked their employees to report to work at 6 p.m. on the days Newtown was scheduled to go off. Which wasn't terribly inconvenient for Maayaa if she could do something with her free days, but her six-year-old Dell Inspiron laptop was in fact a desktop thanks to a faulty battery, and as soon as the lights went off, the laptop died too. Her phone battery could last only four hours, six if she wasn't jumping from one app to the next. Every time the lights went off, a kind of powerlessness crawled into her skin. Everything about Ghana irked her. The traffic, the long queues, the policemen, the price of gas and food, transport fares, older women who didn't know how to mind their business, the blackouts, the politicians who talk on TV like Ghanaians are their spoiled children, the bad roads, the terrible drainage system. She had marched for hours during the dumsor demonstration in May. Seeing hundreds of young people demanding the bare minimum activated the dormant hope lying still in her body. She had ridden on that high for as long as she could, but months after the demonstration the country was still in the same stifling state. She felt suffocated. She was of the generation who would change the stereotyped definition of Ghanaians from laid back to doers, but which for the moment were stuck in 9-to-5 jobs to survive. Jobs that were really 6-to-8 if you counted the time it took to get ready and sit in traffic to make it to work at 9. On Sunday the pastor asked the congregation to pray for the leaders of the country, for God to gift them with divine wisdom.

Bullshit. What they needed to do was flog the hell out of their asses. Maybe, just maybe, that would work.

SECTION B
[50 marks]

Using a photo, illustrate the beginning and end of a relationship. Employ the use of perspective for depth, adequate lighting for warmth, and shadows for illusion.

*You are advised to spend about **a year** on this section.*

Nothing makes faithfulness suspicious like the attention of a handsome man. He tells me in between gasps and contorted movement that I treat his body like I'm madly in love with him; and I want to throw my head back and tell him, of course I am! What do you think this is, an audition for a sex scene? But pausing in the middle of making a man moan to make a speech might interfere with being documented as the best lover anyone ever had. So I stick to the swinging rhythm of making art with spit around skin and pretending to be toothless.

Fifteen minutes later we're breathless, half of his weight on my 75 kilogram body. I expect to suffocate after exactly thirty seconds but there's something comforting in breathing into his shoulder, and when he tries to shift off me to lessen his weight, I readjust myself and sink my teeth gently into his skin, code for "here's your permission, my body is all yours." He gets it because he stays in place. The way loving him makes me happy is almost unhealthy.

Before this, it was the last day of December in Max's house. I had lied to my mother that I was going to church with Enyo to avoid being guilt-tripped into going for another crossover service from 9 p.m. to 2 a.m., which involved half trying to look respectable while chewing gum maddeningly to keep myself and my mother awake, and jumping along with everyone when the clock struck twelve to usher in the New Year. I didn't want to do it again this year, I had done it twenty-six years in a row, and I could skip it this one time without feeling the guilt of God's side-eye. Instead, I agreed to go to a house party with

Ayebea, where we would just chill and dance and drink wine to usher in the New Year. Go ahead, call me a devil, it's just this one time, God will wipe away my sins anyway.

I wore a black skimpy dress that forced my boobs to hug each other in a manner that implied they would definitely be interested in suffocating a lucky chap. But there I was, cuddling a glass of wine, sitting in between a kissing couple and two men arguing about politics.

"Ma guy, Kuffour do in body like e be gentleman but e den in government rob Ghana pass any presido. Make you no do your body like you no hear about the audit report wey dem chop sixty billion cedis of taxpayer's demma money. He come lie we say HIPC good for wonna body but them chop sixty billion. Sixty billion o? Den he sanso open in mouth tell we say corruption be 'as old as Adam' so he no go expose corruption for in government. Chale chale, politicians all demma mordas."

"Chale you for chill, onipa yɛ ade a, ɔsɛ ayeyi. Ebi like you forget Rawlings in time. Rawlings be criminal pass. Kuffour changed the game, let's not deny it. He was the first president to practice an all-inclusive governance. Eno be Kuffour who start National Health Insurance Scheme?"

He shifts his body off the sofa and I get a full look at him. I can already tell from the curry color of his crisp Henley T-shirt that he's a slut. His bald head looks so silky I want to pass my hands over it. It accentuates his beard, which looks so glossy and well-trimmed and midnight black. I imagine his lips taste like the inside of an almost ripe strawberry because, honestly, I don't know what God was thinking giving a boy such pink lips. The whites of his eyes are so clear, I could stare for a good five minutes without getting bored. His gaze meets mine and shame crawls into my cheeks. Because just from that look, he knows that I know that he's good-looking. And I'm embarrassed and convinced that he's now ugly as fuck and I would never be interested in a man who knows he's good-looking anyway.

Despite my pigheadedness and reluctance to open up, by August I have committed the shape of the birthmark inside Sydney's left thigh to memory, and I think it's both funny and weird that he is ticklish only on his right side. I attribute his tendency to overcompensate, competitiveness, and subtle urges to be the smartest in a room to having conventional Christian teachers for parents. And when I found out he lost his virginity at seventeen to his eighteen-year-old chrife girlfriend on a Friday night, who spent the next forty-eight hours locked in a bathroom trying to wash her sins away because she had sinned against God by having sex, and then proceeded to cut him off for an entire year, I understood his desperateness to be overly prepared.

By September I'm spending half of my days in his one-bedroom apartment, he knows all my friends by name, calls my mother twice a month, occasionally plays FIFA with my little brother, and has already picked out the names of the two kids we're going to have when we marry. The two kids who are going to be a perfect blend of his bark-wood skin and my freckled nose, his perfectly lined teeth that are as white as the privilege that cushions generations yet to be born, and my sculpted cheekbones, and most definitely inherit his thick eyelashes and six-foot-two frame, and maybe borrow my full lips.

I am on the phone at his place telling Ayebea we need to riot because why the hell did groceries for two weeks just cost me 267 cedis and how was anyone surviving in this country? She says to me, Maayaa, you're clearly thriving, because my father pays our security guard 350 cedis a month and that man has three kids. I shake my head and tell her I for lef Ghana. Sydney kisses my cheek and whispers in my other ear, "We for lef Ghana." It's not funny but I'm giggling like an idiot.

I'm happy. We're happy. I'm reminded of the night of the house party, responding to him as softly as my wine-drunk self could muster. That yes, "politicians all demma mordas but Kuffour den e government attaché free basic education plus school feeding program give the economy, wey the economy come make bola sef. He san increase the daily wage from 42 pesewas to 2 cedis 50 pesewas. So by all means, demma mordas, but he do som."

We're happy. I'm happy. I'm dating a good-looking man whose ego juts me in the ribs in more ways than I can count. Who never fails to remind me of how great a boyfriend he is. But I'm happy.

So happy I do not panic when my period is twenty-two days late. So happy that when three pregnancy kits from three different pharmacy shops each read positive, I still don't panic. Marie Stopes is thirty-five minutes away from my house, and I have Ayebea and Sydney for emotional support. So so happy,

I wasn't expecting his reaction to me informing him of my intention to abort to be met with anger and accusations of murdering a future.

SECTION C
[50 marks]

Show your readers a present-day moment. In what ways will you ground them in time, space, location, and specificity?

*You are advised to spend **about a week** on this section.*

"Sydney, your sauce is strong because tell me how these niggas swam past my IUD? But praise the Lord, Marie Stopes is stronger." Maayaa laughs. Her laughter is like a sucked-in belly let loose.

"What are you talking about?"

"Oh yeah, I missed my period. You know how I was cranky this entire week and I thought it was my body fucking with me? Turns out a bitch is pregnant. Anyway, is there any chance you can free up your Wednesday morning to go to Marie Stopes with me? I could ask Ayebea but I—"

"You're pregnant?"

"Sydney. Yes, I just said that and—"

"Marie Stopes for what?"

"What do you mean for what? You don't know what happens at Marie Stopes anymore?"

"How are you going to tell me you're pregnant and aborting at the same time?"

"Um . . . I'm confused. As opposed to . . . what? Yaay! I'm pregnant . . . baby shower? Of course I'm aborting, this is hella unplanned. Neither you nor I are prepared for it."

"Yes, I know that. But we can prepare towards it. You haven't even given me time to think about this and you're already scheduling a date to abort? Why are you treating this like it's a casual walk to the station?"

"Because I didn't think this would be something *we* have to think through. And I'm not treating it like it's a 'casual walk to the station.' It's the logical decision."

"We've had several conversations about having kids. I thought we both agreed that we wanted to have two kids."

"Yes, we talked about having kids after marriage, being financially stable, and settled in our own apartment. You currently live in an apartment that I can't do yoga in comfortably without hitting my head. And I share a room with my brother in my parents' house. It's a no-brainer, we're not ready."

"Maayaa, life doesn't always happen as planned. You of all people know that. You have made things work in impossible situations. We will never be fully prepared but we can start from somewhere."

"Start from somewhere? Ah. This is a joke, right? Okay. No. Sydney, first of all, I am not in any way ready to have a child. I'm not psychologically, mentally, emotionally prepared. I literally just started my food business. I haven't even gotten twenty customers yet to think of growing the business and I have to start thinking of a whole other human being? *You* are not ready for a child. You've been working late hours for the last three months in hopes that you will be promoted. Are you going to magically get free time and extra money in the next nine months? I'm so confused, why are we arguing about this?"

"Because I prefer we keep this child. Yes, it will be hard. Everything in this country is hard. Has been hard. Will always be hard. Does that mean the world stops? No. We will figure it out."

"No. Absolutely not. This is the one thing we are not doing. We are not going to argue about bringing a child into the world when we're both highly unprepared in the middle of a never-ending recession in a country that does not give a fuck about its people. You and I were sitting in this room when your aunt called about her friend dying on the operation table because the lights went off in the middle of a surgical operation and the hospital's generator took over twenty minutes to power up. Uh-uh. That's double homicide, I'm not doing it."

"If we want to make a list of everything working against it, we won't finish now. Nobody is fully prepared for a child. All we need to do is work together. We can do this."

"Uh, yeah. That's not happening."

"I don't want you to abort."

"Sorry, it's happening."

"I really think you're rushing this, and you should think about—"

"I have already thought about this, and the answer is Marie Stopes on Wednesday morning."

"I need you to think hard about this, because any decision you make will affect our relationship."

"Oh wow, is that a threat?"

"I'm just saying, this is a decision between two people. It's not right for you to make that decision by yourself."

Maayaa laughs. Her laughter is like the taut skin of a sucked-in belly.

SECTION D
[50 marks]

Based on the current reality of a specific people or place, write a manifesto that is a realistic projection of the future.

*You are advised to spend **all the time you need** on this section.*

Nothing makes progress suspicious like the mouth of a Ghanaian politician. Three months to elections, President Mahama moves from region to region campaigning for his party and soliciting for votes so he can remain in power for another four years. For the seven o'clock news of the local news channel he wears a red T-shirt and sunglasses and smiles so hard throughout the entire period I worry about how his cheeks are holding up. A crowd has thronged through the stadium. The camera zooms out and zooms in and it switches from a blob of pixelated colors to a little girl propped on the shoulders of her father waving at the camera. The president's smiling face comes into focus.

"Tsoooboi!"

"Yie!"

"Tsooboi!"

"Yie!"

"Tsooboi!"

"Buyayayayayaya!"

"The basic things every community needs are water, education, health care, electricity, and roads, and in the past four years, my government has made sure of exactly that. If we've been able to do these for four years then we're fit to do it for the next four years! The first four years was for building the foundation, the next four years is for constructing the building. Have you seen someone build his foundation for another man to come and build his house on it? It's never ever possible. So we've built the foundation, and we know that Ghanaians will give us four more years to build the house on it. Tsoooboi!"

"Yieee!"

After the December elections, another man starts building his house on someone else's foundation.

The cab ride to Marie Stopes is quiet. I can almost hear my school mother's fruity voice listing my qualities six months after being initiated as a *nino* in secondary school. No longer terrified of seniors and sitting on hard cold floors and holding my nose to avoid retching from scrubbing the wooden toilet structures where shit was everywhere but inside the damn hole.

"And here we have Maayaa, sixteen and ripe enough for the crown, skin the color of hazelnut, eyes a puddle of 'you got something to say?,' mind—revolutionary; just look at that body, humans, aren't we utterly blessed?"

I'm twenty-seven and beauty still knows me by name;

my voice is retired but my lips look like dead rose petals pressed into an old book. My smile is the promise of rain showers on a hot day. My dreams are worn-out horses too tired to gallop. I used to be so full of ambition I wanted to save my country. Now I want to be saved from it.

Nobody tells you failure is a kind of revolution too.

hand-me-down

AYEBEA

It is not only Mamaa's genes that have punctuated the geography of Ayebea's face, it is her personality too. Saturday evening and they're glued to the TV watching *The Voice*. Auntie Gifty's son, Jaden, has his audition airing tonight and they don't want to miss it. A white girl with auburn hair and a voice that can swallow her whole has three of the judges hitting their buttons as she finishes her song. Soon it is Jaden's turn. He walks onto the stage, and with a mic and a nervous smile starts to sing.

When his falsetto voice spills out, Mamaa squeals, and so does Ayebea.

He stretches a note; Mamaa and Ayebea simultaneously slap their thighs: Mamaa slaps her left, and Ayebea favors her right.

When he holds a note for a good fifty-six seconds, Mamaa sighs loudly as if she were drinking her own mother's soup.

Ayebea interjects with soft slaps to her thigh, gently snapping her thumb with her other hand. Soon they're both doing all three, moaning, snapping their fingers, and slapping one thigh. But at different times, creating a synchronized cadence.

The pair have the glossy look of mothers and daughters you watch in badly written telenovelas. They could pass for fresh cushiony butter bread, but someone definitely mixed that dough with cadmium, for it had claws.

Mamaa had Ayebea when she was twenty-six, exactly nine months after Emmanuel had married her. The baby wasn't Emmanuel's. In the beginning, there was no reason for Emmanuel to doubt that the baby wasn't his. Ayebea may have looked just like her mother, but she had his brains and his laugh—or so he chose to believe. But it was Emmanuel's cousin Joe, who had traveled from Berlin for the wedding and stayed three weeks before returning, who was the father.

Mamaa knew this. She had spent her pregnancy in anger. Angry at Joe. Angry at God. Angry with herself. But after Ayebea was born all she felt was sadness. At first she tried to hide it. Tried to smile for a man who wanted her enough to commit to a kind of forever. But her sadness was so foggy it wobbled her walk. It confused her, her sadness. It felt illegitimate, like she had no business feeling it when she was the one who had carried an abomination to term. To this day, Mamaa can't tell what possessed her into telling Emmanuel. But who could've imagined they would've turned out like this. That a man's love could be so impenetrable you'd need an excavator to dig through it. So patient, so intentional about courting empathy, he cajoled joy back into her body. Carried her guilt until it became his. Blamed himself for not protecting her well enough, fostered his rage for his cousin only. His love made everything good, turned this child that wasn't his into his alone.

Ayebea knew this too. When she was thirteen she broke into tears and refused to eat for two days. She had spent every day of the last week learning math and holding hands with the boy from next door. Three days after he kissed her on the lips he refused to talk to her. She was inconsolable; you'd think she was newly widowed. Mamaa, having no use for tears unless for future pleasure, scolded her—not for the deed, but for being a crybaby. She dragged her to her room, stripped bare to skin in front of Ayebea, angrily lifted her pale breasts to the ceiling as if in sacrifice, grabbed flesh from backside to inner thighs to calves, and swore furiously: "Men will try to break this body, but remember this body is a god. And gods are fiery, indulgent, self-seeking beings who men have never and will never have control over. So act like it, and only give permission to those who are deserving."

It was the day she learned that her father wasn't her father.

She still called her father "Father," but the way you talk with food in your mouth, content in your gluttony.

After learning this, Ayebea would have a recurring nightmare for several months. A dream in which two sets of well-chiseled hands delicately sawed open her lady parts, and then sewed them back together with a stainless-steel needle and black thread, only to rip them apart all over again. She would

wake up—a wordless scream strangling her throat, and a thirst
hankering at her neck and belly. She had told her mother that
it wasn't the brutishness of the sawing, or the inelegance of the
bastard hands' poor sewing skills, or even the mercilessness in
ripping through the defeated skin.

It was the sheer disbelieve at her own body's inability
to stage a protest, an acutely distressing shock at the flesh's
ability to feel all thousand pins of pain stabbing through it,
even in dreamland, especially in dreamland. Mamaa molded
her daughter's soft body to her bosom; how she wished she
could hold her longer. Something sharp and wretched stung
her chest and she wanted to wring it out. Instead, she offered
her a promise—the flesh may know nothing, but it knows
enough to learn well. From then, Ayebea would wake up after
every nightmare to a flask of warm ginger water to chase the
bad away, and the sound of her father's footsteps crouching her
doorstep. And only then would she fall back to sleep.

There were days where Mamaa worried that her love
wasn't enough to shield Ayebea. But she took comfort in the
little and big victories. Like how unfazed Ayebea was by the
whims of men and how quickly she moved on from their
disappointment. It might have worried her a little bit if that
was all there was to her, but once, over the phone, she heard
her tell her best friend, "Maayaa, it's okay to be sad, don't
pile up guilt on top of your grief. Yes, I know people get
their heart broken all the time. Your sadness doesn't need to
be unique for it to be acceptable. It's okay. And remember

what my dad always says? If a man is not loving you into yourself, drop him fast."

If the mother and daughter loved you, they loved you wide—a bomb blast, confetti at rich people's parties, five million copies of a bestseller, a flight of starlings in a murmuration, all of Agbogbloshie's monthly sewage. The entire purity and filth of the earth was their loving you.

They spoke to both young and old softly, but giving every word the substance of an insult.

It was mesmerizing to watch them unfold—not a plotted wickedness. Not calculated mischief, but free-flowing, innate—dark thoughts burrowed deep within them. What is clear is their cruelty was an effortless switch only they knew the coordinates to.

Perhaps trauma is a leaking faucet that trickles from a twenty-six-year-old raped by her husband's own blood the night after her wedding, or perhaps trauma boils up a storm until a woman's body becomes a confluence for all things savage. Or perhaps there are things neither science nor fiction has articulated—how the gene of perpetual ruthlessness is handed down from bruised mother to product of her pain.

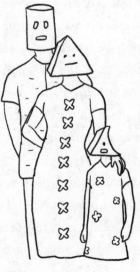

silence

DEANNA

"Does that hurt?"

I want to say "a little" but I'm still half asleep so I garble it in my throat, and Yao gets it because he gently kneads the knots in my shoulders. A strobe of sunlight cuts through the window, illuminating his sandalwood skin—a smooth, polished surface, worthy of the light bouncing off it, thanks to a rich diet of serums and toners and scrubs sponsored by my morning and nighttime skin routines. He smells like the same shea butter + coconut oil + CeraVe + oud oil mixture he's rubbing into my back. I draw circles on his left thigh with my right hand as he holds my body as though he were remolding it into shape. Sat on the bed, I yield my body to him. Loosen it into a foldable thing so he can easily knead the lotion into my skin.

We do this every morning. Yao rubbing lotion on my back had become part of our daily ritual. On the days we went to bed facing in opposite directions and woke up still mad at each other, he did it like it was a job—mechanical, showing up only to get paid. But most days his fingers melted into my skin like he was handling something beloved.

The night Yao proposed, instead of saying yes, I had replied with "Finally, someone to make up for all the years my poor old back has gone unmoisturized." He had laughed that big laugh of his that managed to swallow all other noise and swore to commit to moisturizing my poor neglected back.

"I found your poodle ring."

I froze in mid quarter-circle. He continued kneading, as though he could already sense the tension.

"It was in the old medicine pouch, the one with the expired diazepam."

My frozen body could cut through the silence.

"I left it in there because I didn't want to take it out and lose it. But I've put the medicine pouch on the dining table. Do you want me to put it back in the cabinet?"

"No, please leave it on the dining table," I said back.

On my thirtieth birthday Amoafoa had given me an unexpected gift. A super-cute ring made in the shape of a shiny gold poodle. The ring was made to look like you had a miniature poodle with its paws wrapped around your finger. I had seen a picture of the ring months before on Twitter and sent it to her with all the heart eyes in the world, squealing at the sheer cuteness of it. She had attached a note that said, "I know you currently have your crush goggles on, so Yao is the only cute thing you see, but I hope this ring knocks him off first place just for today." I don't even know where and how she managed to buy that ring but I couldn't have loved her any more.

Apart from a blurry Facebook photo we had both been tagged in, there was nothing to prove that our friendship had ever existed. Not the years of tweeting at and about each other. Not several megabytes' worth of WhatsApp conversations, not the countless selfies we took on her phone (she had the better camera quality) for every second we spent together. Not even a mention of each other's name in our absences. I know this because we had both deleted our social media accounts. Facebook was first to go. And then Twitter (although we started new accounts months later at separate times). And I know from a mutual friend that she lost her phone, and if you know Amoafoa, you know she never backs anything up.

This was someone I knew, as sure as I knew every menstruating month would come with pain, that I was going to love forever.

I knew it within three days of meeting her. We met at the Accra passport office, the one close to Kinbu. I had woken up at 5:30 a.m. just to get ready early enough to get there before 8. I made it at 8:17 and met a queue outside the entrance, long enough to make up a platoon. The entrance was flooded with people. I walked past a chatty group of young women in a blue-and-green African-print uniform with OGASS spelled out in thick black lettering, and joined the queue, standing right behind a bald man in a red long-sleeved shirt. It took a few seconds for it to register but I was both confused and taken aback by his smell. Soon it became clear to me that he had sprayed cologne on without taking a bath, or he had some kind of condition such that no amount of perfume could entirely rid him of the bad smell. I considered going back home for a split second, but my passport was expiring in two weeks; I needed to be done with this. I rummaged through the small leather bag I always carry with me and took out my phone. I had asked for the day off because we all know everything in Ghana civil service works at the speed of a wounded aging snail. And although I was lucky enough to work in a company like TPT that wasn't a pain in the ass, my work bestie absolutely didn't want to go through the workday without me, so she'd asked if I could pass by work anyway if I was done before noon. I took a picture of the queue and sent it to her WhatsApp along with the message "see you before noon GhanaManTime ☺."

The man behind me was chewing gum loudly and furiously, occasionally letting out a loud pop. If he'd been within hearing range of my father's ear, he would've called him a bush girl. Or at least stared him down into confirming his poor manners. Ahead of me, a woman was eating what appeared to be rice and stew in a foam pack. I wondered how hungry she was to be comfortable with standing and eating around several people. I would have been too self-conscious to open the pack of food much less take a bite. The queue had moved much faster than I anticipated and I was almost at the edge of the entrance. *Not so bad, Ghana, shame on me for thinking you're not efficient.* Or so I thought, until I made it past the entrance, only to then be directed to a shed on the left side of the main compound, with thin wooden benches laid out in rows of ten or so, to join yet another queue.

There were at least eighty people before me. I sat on the bench beside an older-looking man and pulled out my copy of *Tar Baby*. I should've taken another book because I was just a few pages away from finishing, but I wanted to be done soon enough so I could discuss the book with my friend from college on his weekend away from parenting. I tried to sit still the first hour, but it was a struggle. A woman was asking someone over the phone to check if the lights were back on. There was no quiet; it seemed as if everyone was having pockets of conversation in not-too-loud but loud-enough-for-me-to-hear voices. Someone sneezed so loud I sprang to my feet, alarmed. And then sat down almost immediately, embarrassed. There was a uniformed security guy who would call the next person into the building every ten to fifteen minutes, and we would mindlessly shift in our seats to get to the front of the line. I would get halfway through a paragraph and then my brain would check out, suddenly distracted by the mosquitoes dancing on the head of the woman two seats ahead of me who kept blowing her nose. I wondered if mosquitoes could catch a cold from sucking the blood of a human with a cold. Would they experience it as just an ordinary cold or would it be too strong for their bodies and instantly kill them? There was just one more row in front of me, then it would be my turn to go in. At 11:57, I bought a bottle of water to quiet my growling stomach. I'd been reading the same page for at least thirty minutes.

Finally, it was my turn. The security guy asked me to walk into the main building and enter the second room on the left, with "No. 2" written on it. I forgot all about the irritation of waiting and picked up my bag. Inside the small room there was another queue, but it was much shorter and there were only three people ahead of me. There was a wooden table in the corner of the room, and a smaller door leading to another office facing us.

"Next!" A voice from the inner room called out. The gentleman closest to the front got up and entered the room. In less than ten minutes he was out. After two more shouts of "Next!" I entered the room. Before the words "good morning" could roll out of my mouth like a good Ghanaian citizen, the woman shook her head at me.

"Young lady, you can't take a passport picture with this hair," a burnt-almond-colored woman with three brisk tribal marks on each cheek said to me in heavily accented English.

I was wearing an auburn fringe bob wig that I knew made me look extra cute, as God is my witness. She could see the confusion on my face.

"Your hair color has to be the same color as your natural hair color." What has that got to do with taking a picture for my passport, for god's sake? I thought to myself.

"Were you born with this red or wine hair? What color sef is this your wig?"

"But . . ."

"You have to take the wig off o, my sister. I don't make the rules."

There was no way I was taking my headshot without my wig. I looked like a mad angry woman with my almost two-week cornrows underneath that wig.

"Young women of today dɛ you like life paa o. Your wig mome is nice but it has to be black. You can't take it off, eh?

I was too angry to say anything, so I just shook my head.

"You step outside for now and do something about your hair and then come back wae. Next!"

I clutched my bag and walked out of the inner room, and outside of the main room into the hallway. I felt completely stupid and was seconds away from crying right there in the hallway. That is when I saw her coming from room No. 1. Her skin was the first thing I noticed. Her brown pupils contrasted her dark skin beautifully. She had on yellow-rimmed glasses that I instantly liked, a coffee-brown fitting dress, and a black wig pulled into a ponytail. I remember thinking if I had her skin I would always wear bright colors just so I could announce myself. Her front teeth were slightly protruding, as though God deliberately arranged the front row of her teeth as a bulging arc. I could tell she had gone to a great deal to hide the acne under her eyes. She wasn't skinny, but she wasn't big either.

She looked at me and knew right away.

"Do you need a black wig? You can have mine, I just finished taking my headshot." Her voice was a soft thing, a stringed instrument playing a distance away.

"Oh God, yes, I do. Thank you so much. I was this close to tears because they won't let me take mine in this colored wig."

"Yeah, they're annoying. If it is a prerequisite, they should have it clearly on that terrible website before booking appointments."

It was a little too big for my head but it was far better than my messy cornrows. She offered to hold on to my bag and my wig, waited for me outside of room No. 2 until I was finished, and then helped me put my wig back on.

"I don't know what I would have done without you. Thank you . . . ?"

"Amoafoa. And don't mention, it's been my pleasure."

"Amoafoa, that's a very beautiful and unique name. I'm Deanna."

"Aw, thanks! You have a beautiful name too."

"Oh please. If all the names in the world were competing for plain, Deanna will be in the top ten. My typical Akyem parents had no business naming me Deanna."

She laughed and we made our way outside the building. I expected it to end just there, a friendly encounter with a stranger who had been more than kind. Maybe we would exchange numbers but I wasn't really expecting it to go anywhere, especially when I found out her age. I was twenty-seven; I had no expectations of being friends with a just-turned twenty-year-old. But it didn't end there. She was driving a blood-red Hyundai Accent and refused to take no for an answer to her dropping me off, despite my house being completely out of her way. She cleared the front seat of books, a disorganized pile of printed sheets, and a big gold necklace that looked like it was handed down from at least three generations before her.

She drove cautiously and was a little too close to the steering wheel and holding on to it as if for dear life. I wondered if I was making her nervous or if she was just a nervous driver. She reached for a Tic Tac from the center console just as I was reaching into my bag for my phone. Our elbows grazed each other, and I smiled awkwardly at her.

I found out her name was Amoafoa Ankonam Kurabi and couldn't hide my surprise at Ankonam being her given name.

"I know. I know. People always assume it's a name I gave to myself out of sheer dramatics, so I rarely actually tell people about that name, I always use my initials instead. I'm not even sure why I'm telling you. I guess it's because I like you." We both smiled.

"But yes, my mother named me Ankonam because my father died three months before I was born, and my then broken-hearted mother, burdened with the weight of aloneness in the journey to single-parenting, named me Ankonam to mark her circumstance."

We talked about her rich stepfather, who married her mother when Amoafoa was two years old, and how that changed their lives forever. How much she loved him, and even though she never got to meet her father, sometimes felt guilty she had more affection for her stepfather. We talked about how she still remembered bits of her childhood before her mother remarried.

We talked about my parents too. How I absolutely and completely loved my father, and how my mother felt like a stranger to me, how I didn't really feel like I knew her.

She was in her second year in university, studying for a Bachelor of Arts in Integrated Rural Art and Industry, and was equal parts confused and impressed with how I, an English major and an M. Phil. English holder, ended up working as a comms and development manager for an urban planning research startup. We talked about my love for dogs and her absolute hatred of them. About long church services and why every pastor in this country was convinced God was hard of hearing with all their needless shouting. About books and literature and how poetry did nothing for her, or at least all the old-white-men poems she'd read so far. How she screamed delightfully when she found out I was five pages away from finishing *Tar Baby*, and made me promise we would discuss it the second I was finished with it. About the smell of hospitals, six reasons I liked the color black, how quickly she spun an entire scenario about a dream wedding in Saudi Arabia to a Saudi prince because she received a scam WhatsApp message in Arabic from a foreign number. My subsequent request for a free ticket, a cute Saudi Arabian to escort me everywhere during the wedding, and gold necklaces and silk laces to stunt on invisible hoes. We laughed and giggled and talked about so much in that forty-minute ride you would think we had known each other for years. When she dropped me in front of my peeling-paint wooden gate, after we had exchanged numbers and already sent an initial hi, just after I had thanked her profusely for saving my day and going beyond to drop me off at home, she told me with a smile in her voice:

"I suspect we're going to be best friends. I don't care. I don't care. I've already decided."

"Right after I coerce you into loving dogs and poetry," I tell her, shutting the door gently with the biggest smile on my face.

There was a time when Yao had teased, cajoled, pushed for me to initiate another conversation with Amoafoa, had even been forceful. But my last three reactions had been such a whirlwind of emotions that he'd resolved to treat the topic with a guarded tenderness or complete silence.

"You good?" I could tell he was being cautious.

I look at his nose. Search inside the dark maze of his nostrils, glad that Nhyira inherited his pinched jutting nose that made his face synonymous with regality. I stare at the tiny birthmark that could pass for a map of Accra above his upper left lip. We joked that if he sneezed just a little harder, he could shift the position of his map-birthmark to another region. Every time I look at it, I have an innate desire to lick it off his face.

"My dad is getting Nhyira today. I already told his teacher so she's aware." I distract myself with the day's events. You think a father's love is boundless and then they become grand-fathers whose entire lives revolve around their grandchildren. We lived at least an hour away thanks to Accra's horrendous traffic, but my dad still managed to spend at least one day out of the week helping out with my kids.

"You good?" He ignores me and repeats himself, this time palming my face.

"Yeah. I am."

"You're sure?"

"Yeah, let's talk about it in the evening. I have to get ready for work."

"All right. I love you. Don't starve yourself or nibble on food today, please. Eat like you know I can't live without you."

"I will. I already ordered Rockstone's waakye for lunch." I tiptoe to kiss him.

Amoafoa was the quaintest twenty-year-old I had ever met. She spoke three Ghanaian languages and understood enough Yoruba to know when she was being insulted and how to insult you back. She enjoyed cooking but only if someone else did the shopping. She had picked up so many art hobbies—photography, painting, pottery, soap making, candle making. Hell, she once spent seven weeks in a carpentry shop because she wanted to learn how to make a coffee table from scratch. Her parents, convinced she wanted to be an artist, pushed her to do an art-related course and she ended up studying integrated rural art and industry at KNUST. But what she really wanted to do, she told me, was "to be a good audience. An observer of art, but not just any random observer, one who understands the art enough to know its execution and function." She had a fear of living a too-small life, was waiting for a version of her body that she could fall madly in love with, and a handsome man who thought she shat gold. I found her overall demeanor very idealistic, but it didn't bother me too much because she was young and still had time to discover herself.

Our relationship wasn't a slow bloom; if anything there was a boundless fondness steaming off our heads, the affection we shared escaping like vapor from a pressure cooker. Our friendship blossomed from the very beginning. It was like knowing you love someone even before getting to know them, and so when you did get to know them you spent the rest of your time dishing out all the love you had for them.

We gave each other books and discussed characters and authors as though there was a likelihood of meeting them at the Nubuke Foundation. We both read *Blackass* and thought Igoni Barrett had a beautiful mind. I found the main character's reaction when he woke up and realized that he was no longer a black person a little unusual—almost irritating—how he didn't freak out, wasn't visibly surprised, and just went straight ahead into planning his next move. She explained softly that Igoni picked the story's foundation from Kafka's "Metamorphosis" and needed the story to go elsewhere; an element of surprise would've dragged the story in a different direction, and might have made him call in his family, while much of the story was based on the fact that he wanted to stay hidden from his family.

I sent her poems that made me happy poets existed, and she liked Dorothea Lasky's "Porn" so much she was both blown away and inspired to search for more poetry. We both reinvented memories—I turned pleasant memories into even happier ones, just so I could continue remembering them, hold on to them longer. She reinvented awkward and cringeworthy memories into good ones, which I thought was an

excellent coping mechanism except she always ended up
feeling guilty about them. She felt greedy and dishonest, as
though she were polishing a thing she had no right to polish.
But they're your memories, I told her, *who better to polish them
than you?*

She couldn't wait to move out and live on her own.
I wished my parents' house could still accommodate me so I'd
have less anxiety about rent money.

She watched Kumawood because she wanted to be patri-
otic and support Ghana, and said I needed to be a good citizen
too and watch it with her.

I loved almost everything about her expect the relationship she had with her body.

I swear to God I thought she was beautiful. And I'm not
saying this just because she's my friend.

There are several people who aren't exactly the type you
see and swoon over, but Amoafoa was certainly not one of
them. She was striking in an unusual way. First, she had skin
to die for. Everyone and their mama in this country is dark-
skinned but that girl is blackity black. The kind of black Anish
Kapoor would want to purchase artistic rights to and keep
to himself. If I came out with skin like hers nary a person
would I respect. Her skin alone was license to claim everlasting
beauty. I wished she would just leave her face alone and stop
putting every goddamn solution on it to cure the acne, but
she had a beautiful face, her square nose held her frames in
place like it was made just for that, even her protruding teeth,
which she detested so much, were such a perfect complement

to her jawline. As if God knew well enough to angle the
contents in her mouth such that speaking would flex the jaw
muscles into perfection.

But alas, she was insecure about her body. Picking at her
face, hiding in clothes that made her blend in, fade out, become less visible. In late May, three weeks after she had turned
twenty-two, we were having lunch in a newly opened rooftop
restaurant and she was wearing the algae-green one-hand dress
with sunflower pattern embroidered at the intersection of the
shoulder blade that I had given to her for her birthday. She
looked lovely and two women had already complimented her
before we took our seats. I had taken at least a dozen pictures
of her and we were chowing down our food. She was telling
me about a book she bought the weekend before that was so
badly written she wanted to find the author and beat her to
death with her copy. I was laughing so hard I was worried I'd
choke on my food. I didn't realize the man in the navy striped
suit was coming to our table until he stopped right beside me
and leaned over.

"Hi, you're very beautiful. I just wanted to come over and
say that. I hope you enjoy the rest of your evening."

Because I didn't see him coming towards us, it took me a
second too long to say thank you, and by then he had turned
to walk away.

Amoafoa giggled with food in her mouth. She had initially
placed her purse on the table, and she moved it under her chair
to make more room for her arms.

"Fine fine girl, look how men are going out of their way to compliment you."

"Oh, please." I laughed and switched back to the subject of the book.

"What was so bad about the book?"

She took her time to chew her food before answering.

"I wonder what it feels like to be considered pretty by everyone."

"Ah, Amoafoa, what are you talking about? Didn't two women just call you lovely? Because a random man called me pretty now I'm considered pretty by everyone?"

"But you are pretty!"

"And so are you!"

"Yeah, well, not as pretty as you." She was breaking off a portion of salmon like it was the hardest job in the world.

"Don't be silly. You are pretty and I am pretty. There are no greater thans or lesser thans."

"Not true. You find me beautiful only because you love me."

"That is absolutely not true. I thought you were a beautiful girl the minute I set eyes on you and I didn't even know you then to love you."

"Deanna, I'm not saying I'm ugly or not beautiful. I'm just saying you are pretty without effort. You use very little makeup, I use an insane concoction and mixture of things to hide my black spots. Yeah, I can be pretty but it is with a lot of effort." She reached for a tissue and gently dabbed at her face as if to prove her point.

"Amoafoa, you know that the only reason I use little makeup is because I suck at it. You *know* that, you've seen me try and laughed at me several times. And you obsess over your barely noticeable black spots but you look gorgeous even without makeup. Why are we even having this argument?" The high pitch my voice had taken was betraying me.

"Again, I'm not saying I'm ugly, I just want you to admit that you're prettier than me. I'm not saying I'm not pretty too, but in the name of conventional beauty, or even just the simple math of greater than, it is evident to anyone who has eyes that you are prettier than me."

"In the name of conventional beauty? Who decides conventional beauty? Men? You're telling me one man telling me I'm beautiful is weightier than two women going out of their way to call you beautiful? The male gaze is your highest marker of beauty now?"

"You're intellectualizing this. I just wanted to make a simple point of how good it must feel to be sure of your beauty." She sounded upset.

"Okay."

Now we were both upset, sitting in our individual feelings of discontent with each other. She tried to steer the conversation back to the bad book. How the characters were drawn out like Africans on display, wearing clothing strictly as an identifier for African as if it made perfect sense to be wearing an agbada on a lazy Saturday afternoon in your own home, and speaking in jaunty exaggerated sentences like they couldn't be Africans if they didn't sprinkle at least three *oooh*s and *ahh*s and *ewoo*s in their sentences. But the air had already been sullied with our argument. I could only manage short responses and I couldn't muster the excitement to finish my meal. Dinner ended early and we parted ways.

We didn't talk the next day, or the day after, or the next. I saw her tweet twice, and each time it made me angrier. I felt I was owed an apology, but even as I sat in my anger, I knew my irritation was no match for her low self-esteem. I felt burdened by the responsibility of being the older one. It wasn't how weighed down she was by her low self-esteem that bothered me as much as her need to make a comparison of us to fuel her unbelief in her own beauty.

How she managed to be both unparalleled in brilliance and frenzied in self-deprecation made me want to pull my hair out. I waited seven days with no message or call from her, and then bought cupcakes from her favorite cake store, passed by her house after work on a Friday, and we pretended like nothing had happened. When I think back, this was the beginning of our breaking. How long silences followed every disagreement. How anxiety and resentment filled up the silences, and how I translated every one of her silences into blocks of rejection.

I really love my job. I really like that I get to be a comfortable anomaly. Because really, how many public universities in Ghana introduce new courses that exist strictly as an experiment for how fluidly the humanities can intersect and coexist with the sciences, and then build a small team around it just to test it? The plan had been to teach in the English Department, but after working in TPT it made absolute sense to me that all the core fields in academia had to be looked at through a humanities lens, and luckily for me, the dean, bless her wooden but adventurous heart, decided to give me a semester to test it out, and here we are four semesters later. So anyway, as I was saying, I really like my job, but goddamn, sometimes I read an essay so bad that I want to print it out, scrunch it up into a ball, and feed it to the student spewing garbage with such confidence. I look up from my computer and tell my colleague Lydia this. She looks at me weirdly like I just confessed a murder. I miss Amoafoa; she would've understood my humor.

Lunch announces itself even before the delivery guy gets to our office door. I can smell the sweet aroma of the waakye just as he knocks. There's a kitchen but I don't want to move from my desk so I make space and layer the surface with an old red napkin. I catch a glimpse of my gut in my computer screen. I can't believe I wanted to have three kids. With which body? After two big-headed babies, I've moved from a size 6 to a 10, and three years later, I'm still struggling to lose the baby weight. Never again.

My phone vibrates. It's Yao.

"I'm eating like I know you can't live without me and will absolutely go nuts if I leave you alone with Nhyira for more than seventy-two hours."

His big laugh warms my belly.

I had been seeing Yao for just a little over four months when Amoafoa started having boy trouble. She used to tease me all the time because I was very hesitant about dating again. Even laughed at me because an acquaintance had told me one

time I was too old to be heartbroken, and I had taken that shit
to heart. Before Yao, I had been single for so long I wasn't
sure I remembered how to operate a French kiss, but now the
thought of him as a fixture in my life was almost seamless.
Amoafoa was in her third year and dating a boy from one of
her classes called Maloney, which I thought was an odd name
for such an ordinary boy. I immediately knew it wouldn't last
because he acknowledged their relationship only when they
were alone. And yet one Thursday at 2:43 a.m. I was woken
up by an inconsolable and distraught Amoafoa, who somehow wanted me to stop Maloney from breaking up with her.
(All because he met me once and was seemingly impressed
that Amoafoa had older working friends?) I didn't know how
to do that and I didn't want to do it even if I knew how. So
instead, I stayed on the phone with her until she eventually
fell asleep from crying too hard. How we both survived her
relationship failure was a goddamn miracle because the entire
time I wanted to slap both Amoafoa and Maloney. Amoafoa
for holding on to that bottom-barrel mediocrity of a relationship as though its existence was evidence of her relevance.
Maloney for his lack of tact and sheer existence.

A month after their breakup, my company won a bid for
an urban planning contract in Nairobi, and to reward us for
the hard work we put in we were given two days off. I was
ecstatic: 1. I needed a day to myself to stay in bed and do
nothing, and 2. I needed to spend more time with Amoafoa,
at least a full day. Because even though it seemed she'd gone
past the threshold of despair in the breakup process, and she

had promised me she'd stopped texting Maloney incessantly, it was hard to fully gauge where she was emotionally. So I went over with two movies saved on a drive, ate yam and garden egg stew her mother made, and lay beside her on her bed as we watched the movies. Her mother needed help with something so we paused the movie and I spread my arms on the bed as though they were wings. I heard a phone vibrate. Both our phones were next to the pillow, and I couldn't tell which phone made the sound so I checked both. I had no notifications, but she did. A message from Maloney.

What I did next, I'm not proud of, but at the time, I felt it wasn't a big deal because we knew the password to each other's phone. I didn't think I was entirely being nosy. I opened the message and read through almost ten days of messages between her and Maloney. She had been texting him every single day. Begging him to see her for an in-person conversation. He had even blocked her but unblocked her just to tell her to stop emailing him. I felt a deep disappointment and a secondhand embarrassment so fierce my chest hurt. I put the phone back and sat on the bed.

Ten minutes later she came back into the room smiling.

"I hope you didn't watch without me?"

"You told me you had stopped texting Maloney." I spoke slowly, as if each word was shifting something in my chest.

She stopped in the middle of the room, using her big toes to trace the dark gray jagged lines on her white porcelain floor.

"He sent a message while you were gone. I was a little surprised to see his name, so I opened the message."

She tightened the band holding her braids up even though it didn't need tightening. I moved from the middle of the bed to the edge.

"What are you doing to yourself, Amoafoa? He blocked you and you sent him several emails?"

"You had no right to go through my messages." She finally spoke.

"I know and I'm sorry." I could hear her mother from the hallway, speaking to someone on the phone in a voice that could carry on a conversation with a plant. I searched Amoafoa's face for something, shame maybe. But she only looked like she was about to cry.

"I just want closure. I deserve that at least. I just want to have a conversation."

"You want closure from someone who wasn't decent enough to not dump you over text?"

"You don't just get up and break up with someone for no reason." She stared at her feet. "The least he can do is tell me why. I deserve to know why."

"If we all got what we deserved the world would look very different." I shook my head. "Just the other day you were telling me how cringy it was for you to see one of your course mates standing outside her ex's class with a handwritten sign full of questions . . ."

"That's different, she cheated, I didn't do anything."

"The meaning of closure doesn't change to suit your needs."

"I just want to have one conversation with him."

"And he doesn't. So now what? You're just casually going to write yourself as the psycho ex-girlfriend in someone's romantic history? You're not acting smart at all. This boy now has a thread of you consistently leaving unwanted messages. What if he puts it online or something? Does that not worry you at all?" What I really wanted to say to her was that she was being incredibly stupid. But I held myself back.

She cleared the heap of clothes from the plastic chair in her room, sat on it, and proceeded to ignore me. So we sat in silence till finally I had to leave.

The day after she said nothing. So I said nothing too. I had already said enough. The silence sat like an unmovable stone between us. And we walked carefully around it, occasionally chipping at it with small and random and seemingly important news. My itch to take on new risks. A funny tweet she saw. A song I discovered. A beautiful picture of the sunset she took.

When we began dating, Yao and I talked a lot on the phone. Too much, in fact. His work schedule was brutal and confined him to the screen for hours, so we saw each other only once a week, sometimes two. I started shifting my work hours around ever so slightly, working extra hours so I could clock out of work at noon on one Friday out of the month, to be able to spend a weekend with him. I planned for these weekends together to be almost romantic, idyllic maybe, or at the very least, dreamy. It was rarely that—we spent most of them talking, eating, and sleeping till noon, or he listened as I obsessed over my relationship with Amoafoa.

He listened to me talk about things past and new. How a

recent silence reminded me of an older one. How some bled and folded into each other. How my words carried weight only when they were regurgitated by the mouth of a boy. Sometimes I wanted him to interrupt, take sides even, but he mostly listened.

I worried that my preoccupation with the forced quietude in Amoafoa's and my relationship would spill over into my relationship with Yao and stain the harmony we had going on. So I overcompensated with cautiousness, attempted to teach him how to fill up any spaces that popped up between us with anything but silence. But he didn't need a lesson, and thought I was the one who needed one.

"Have you considered that maybe you're softer with me than you are with Amoafoa?" he said to me one night after a familiar rant.

"I *am* soft with Amoafoa."

"Yes, you are . . . but you do get impatient, and you're harsh on her sometimes." He's holding my hand in his palm, slowly massaging the center with his thumb.

"Somebody has got to be honest with her, Yao."

"Yes, and I know you look out for her only because you care about her. But just because you're right doesn't mean it always demands to be said. Truth doesn't always have to be surrounded by an air of urgency."

I say nothing. He takes my other hand and proceeds to massage it too.

"If you'll be willing to accept that you're softer with me, then perhaps you should consider accepting that Amoafoa is more accommodating of the men in her life, maybe too accommodating, that all she has after dealing with them is silence?"

I shake my head, wondering how I could clarify over and over with layers of language, and still be misunderstood.

The day Amoafoa and Opoku met, we were supposed to be out together. Gallery 1957 was launching a new exhibition and we had planned to go together. But I had gotten malaria the week before and was still feeling weak, even though I had finished taking the course of medication. He found her in front of his favorite artwork from the exhibition and they spent the rest of the show talking about art. After a few dates, he asked her to be his girlfriend.

My memory of their relationship in the beginning is like a fog—I didn't think too much of it, mostly because I thought she was still grieving her last relationship, and this was just a distraction to make it easier. Plus, I had been waiting for a good time to tell her I had gotten the lecturer position in Senegal, for which I had been interviewing for weeks now. And I had only a month to move.

When I did finally meet Opoku, he seemed like a decent guy and was visibly taken by Amoafoa, although I worried that she suddenly seemed very clingy and dependent. Changing her entire wardrobe to clothes he liked. Waiting for his approval before getting a particular meal or outfit or even going out. As though she woke up and discovered a symbiotic cord that required her to ask for his permission before doing the littlest of things and needed his validation to be happy. But it was a new relationship, still in its honeymoon phase, so I thought it would ease into something more suitable for both of them.

But she looked happier, sounded more confident, like her voice could fill a small room. She sent more selfies, wore more color, went on a diet to try to lose weight.

"Opoku said I need to lose just a little weight and I'll be perfect."

"Okay, but you're perfect even now."

"Yes, but more perfect." She giggled. She said he made her feel like she was the prettiest girl in the world. And lately she liked looking at herself in the mirror; she never even realized she had such beautiful skin.

It annoyed me that the beauty I swore she possessed, the beauty she assumed she didn't possess, was illuminated through a man's gaze. It wasn't a love gaze, couldn't be, because I too loved her an ocean.

I looked at her smiling face, succumbed to silence, and hugged her.

"That's a very cute ring. Where did you get it? I have a friend who will love it!"

"Oh . . ." I forgot I had put my poodle ring on my little finger until Lydia asked.

"Um, it was a gift from a long time ago."

I want to take it off, but I don't want to lose it again.

Our relationship didn't erode right away. It wasn't a big rot or a rude awakening. It crept in while our lives carried on.

The first year after I moved to Senegal, we were emailing each other every other day.

Long and random and detailed and funny and revealing emails.

I would tell her everything, from the color of my new flat to how good the mangos over here were, the new friend I had made in town, and when Yao moved to Senegal with me since he was working remotely anyway.

She told me everything, how she was terrified of entering her final year because she truly didn't have a clue what came next, to learning how to use the public transport because she'd lent her car to Opoku, new poetry books she'd discovered, arguments with her mother.

Occasionally we would argue about something. Her skipping more than one class to meal prep for Opoku. Me choosing to have a court wedding in Senegal. An expensive gift. A forgotten memory. Big things, small things, and everything in between. And each one was followed by big and long silences. Silences that I always interrupted with a throat clearing.

But eventually I got tired of it. So I let the silence sit.

I intended for it to sit just a little longer, float around, find its way into her throat, and throttle the discomfort or pride or whatever it was that sat there. But the silence made itself comfortable. And one week turned into one month, and one month turned into three. And when next we said hi to each other, the awkwardness of it felt like a fresh wound. So we let the silence sit even more.

And soon enough, the thing we called friendship had shaped itself into a memory.

Friendship is hard when it has ended but you're the only one who doesn't know it, so you start thinking the person is trying to harm you with their absence when they've really moved on, and you're the only one left standing wondering what's happening, wondering if you're doing too much or too little.

Yao worked remotely with an international company that was testing out a four-day work week. I was completely envious of him but also glad because it meant he picked up Nhyira from school three times a week, and my dad took over from us for one day, which meant I only had Tuesdays to pick him up.

I wasn't sure who I would end up with, or even if I'd marry at all. But I always thought it would be someone brainy and funny for sure, a writer maybe, but I didn't think I'd end up with an engineer. Unlike Amoafoa, who ended up with an artist.

I found out from a mutual friend that she had gotten married to Opoku last year and one of her cousins had been her maid of honor. If you'd told the past me that I wouldn't be in the pictures for Amoafoa's wedding I would've straight up called you a hater. I was supposed to help pick out her colors. I would've approved one wedding gown design from her top three. We would've scouted Accra for a wedding planner who wouldn't give us palpitations with poor delivery. Hell, I was supposed to be her maid of honor. But even I can admit it's pretty awkward to ask someone you haven't spoken to in years to be your maid of honor. *Mayday* is used only when everyone's aware you're in distress.

Whenever we went to Ghana, I avoided seeing Amoafoa. Sometimes I wondered if she thought of me, what images of our friendship crossed her subconscious, and whether she occasionally ferried an iteration of us into her dreams. We had stopped texting altogether; she had taken weeks to reply to my last message. It wasn't even how long she took to reply, it was the short sentences and the politeness. I think that was the thing that hurt the most, that she built a web of distance with a painful politeness despite my efforts, but she would cry a fucking river for just about any twat of a man. Yes, I had my faults, I too made silence a god. Spun it into a sublime descent thinking it would make us uncomfortable enough to push us into the limelight. I too rewrote and misread our friendship into an unwanted version. But at least I fucking showed up, didn't I?

this bizarre middleness

TAKYI

Everybody who has been in Takyi's life has heard of this at least three times. Not that it is particularly essential to this story, but it being your first time encountering him and seeing as I am not exactly keen to spare you (after all, it's not as if I know you from Jack), you too shall hear it.

According to Takyi, his father is of the lineage of Kwao Amanor, leader of the glorious Amanokrom (although if you ask me, I don't know what is glorious about them, unless you're counting how well they can mock you while simultaneously being polite), and nephew of Nana Safori (the very first Okuapemhene to be crowned), who led the battalion of the Twifo Asafo against the oppressive rule of the Akwamus, and ultimately led to their freedom.

Why do I know this? Because Takyi talks about it like he was in the fucking room when Osagyefuo asked Nana Safori to lead the Twifo Asafo into war. He narrates it like he was on the battlefield in 1730, smeared in clan symbols and covered in fifty amulets. Talmbout "You for know say my guy Nana Safori na e be guy pass! Guy for the highest order! E never dey back down! E fi collect bullet for en chest wey e naa go sa remove am like e be small ting. Ma guy that. E be guy fokn! Da be my great-great-great-grand-uncle, so you for know sey my blood be correct! What dey wey I no get? Bravery, e dey for my blood inside. Intelligence? E dey for my blood inside! Fine fine boy? I gat this!"

To which he always ended with a hearty victorious laugh as if he'd conquered something. But both he and I know that he ain't really gat this. In fact, he is smack right in the middle of excellence and unremarkability. Like a single grain of sand stuck in the belt of an hourglass. If it is possible for anyone to look 50 percent attractive and 50 percent mundane, such that the mash-up of these two qualities leaves him a right measure of good-looking enough to be liked, and a right measure of ordinariness enough to be looked over—*that* would be Takyi. His entire life is marked by this halfway absurdity: his grades throughout school were good enough to pass classes, but never great enough to be close to the list of intelligent or even above-average boys in the class. His salary—good enough to take care of all his monthly needs and then some, not great enough to save 20 percent monthly. His rule was always, if I can't save just 20 percent, I might as well finish it. Even his penis has been affected by this bizarre middleness—it isn't a huge piece of thing that can be used to hit the heads of women, it's just the right size of averageness. Yet eight out of ten times, he lasts for about six minutes. He, of course, always tells the women that their wet magical cities are responsible for his overexcitement. Between you and me, he wishes he could go fifteen minutes or more.

He likes to blame this comme-ci-comme-ça-ness on his father for falling for his mother. It has nothing to do with her in particular (he loves his mother very much), it has to do with the fact that she comes from a lineage of unambitious men. He doesn't hold it over his father's head too much though, because one look at his mother's backside and everybody understands the old man's fixation. There are a lot of things to be upset about with the old man—like how he is an excellent giver to everybody but his nuclear family. Let any Ama and Kojo from next door or town ask Takyi's father for anything, and suddenly, he's the provider of the year. Most generous-to-strangers, most greasing-the-palm-of-every-outsider. Mr. "you have a roof over your head and everything you'll ever need, extra money for what?" The only difference between him and Ebenezer Scrooge was that he reserved his stinginess for his family. Sometimes Takyi wonders how his mother feels. How she's managed to stay in love with a man who she knew gave freely. Who she saw people praise into godliness for his giving heart, but the generous hands struggled to reach her and her children.

Takyi is a much happier person now that it is just him and the parents at home—all his three siblings left home to start their own families. This was the perk of being the last-born child. It didn't matter that he was thirty-two. In fact, most days he couldn't believe he was thirty-two. When he was little he used to think when people in their thirties walked, their bones creaked in anticipation of arthritis. But here he was, baby boy of life, comfortably living in his father's house, thankful to the gods of all things sensible that the one thing his father did right was to build a house in the city of Accra. Because rent in this city is a punch people keep stomaching just to last long enough in the ring. He couldn't imagine having to contribute rent, even though it made him feel very responsible; he was already pressed as it was that he was paying for utility bills and buying groceries for the house monthly—his mother's way of calling him the man of the house. He was just thankful his operations manager job at Kasapreko Drinks came with a company car, because the price of a brand-new car would set his middle-class ass on perpetual fire.

Still, sometimes he wishes his father had worked harder, you know? Wishes he had been ambitious enough to scoop them out of the middle-class section. Because we all know being part of the lower middle class is just another way of being fashionably poor—one emergency away from being broke. He catches himself daydreaming about a world in which he was born rich, a Honda Civic SI as a present from the parents on his fifteenth birthday, closet bursting with so many clothes his mother gives some away to poorer families every quarter of the year, and sampling a variety of dishes every month because rich Ga women not only have the sweetest tooth, but also have the tendency to make sure the entire neighborhood knows about this acquired taste.

A boy can dream.

Instead, until he was twenty-four, 90 percent of his wardrobe was hand-me-downs. It's a wonder his sister Nana Akua managed to look feminine enough to attract men, much less find one to marry her—because they both wore shirts and shorts after the older two had outgrown them.

Cursed by this same middleness all his life; pegged between the lines of mediocrity. That is, until he met Coleen. To this day, he still can't believe she agreed to be his girlfriend. I'm not one to adhere to only what's possible but I agreed with him on this one. Because if Coleen is the EPL, then Takyi is the boy who watches the match outside the window of a stereotypical African village on the days the electricity company decides to behave. I'm not even exaggerating, you should've seen Coleen. The honey of her skin was a golden glow—most likely a product of being born to a Fante father and a Wulensi mother. (To be very honest, Akan men are the slyest motherfuckers! To bag a woman all the way from the north? Walahi!) That girl's skin looks like she came out photoshopped the professional way, while the rest of us have to contend with pores the size of nostrils. You would think the abundance of hair on a girl would make her less attractive, but there was something, there was just something about her that made a man pay more attention. There would've been nothing spectacular about her eyes except her cornea looped in three different shades of brown, and if Takyi wasn't my homeboy that alone would honestly count for witchcraft. Her boobs weren't huge, not small small, they were like two minutes away from a B cup and chockablock of excitement.

The only thing close to average about Coleen was her ass, which was sizably shaped, nothing too monstrous. But even that was glorious. Girl had an ass with the texture of soft bread baked in 2087 with an 808 bass sound to it. I still don't know how they ended up together. It may very well have been because of Takyi's dedication to being a youth programs organizer at the Bethel Methodist Church. But still, I don't know what showing up to church every Thursday and Sunday, doing your necessary duties and praying like you're good homies with Jesus, has to do with getting a girl like Coleen. All the same, they became a couple in June 2017. And all would've been perfect, except our beautiful Coleen, light-skin goddess, was on a new journey of second chances—which embodied everything, from her mind, to her soul, to her body. And so, at the time Coleen and Takyi started dating, Coleen was a secondary virgin.

You see, our good sister Coleen, prior to Takyi, had dated Eugene, who not only savaged her virginity like a priced delicacy, but overwhelmed her so much that she lost her way in Christ. And so in an attempt to return to her savior, she entrenched herself so deeply in Christ that now a man would have to go through Christ to get to her (and all the spam Christianly messages you see African mothers sharing via WhatsApp broadcast), and just like that—a secondary virgin was born.

Now, even I know that not in a million years would that have worked. Man like Takyi, who takes every opportunity to turn everything into a sexual innuendo, someone who lost his virginity when he was thirteen to his auntie's twenty-one-year-old maid, and has never stopped having sex since then. Abstinence? Throw your head back and laugh with me, beloved.

But so smitten was he by Coleen that he agreed to these terms. Agreed to love Jesus and her more than his orgasms. My man didn't speak two sentences without Coleen's name in his mouth. *Coleen laughs like a balloon deflating. Did you know Coleen was a preemie? Ah chale, you know say na Coleen be assistant school prefect for secondary school? Oh yeah, Coleen is seriously considering sister locs, that girl will look good in anything so I don't even mind. Do you by any chance know a teacher in any of the public schools? Coleen wants to donate some books. Oh chale, Ayorkor, Coleen says I should take your corned beef stew recipe because she really enjoyed what we had at your birthday dinner.* After a few weeks, we were all tired of hearing of Coleen. Takyi would meet with his friends Ayorkor and Naana on Wednesdays for drinks at the Republic Bar, listen to them whine about boy troubles and how deeply fucked society was by its patriarchal vein that it all felt hopeless. Drink two mugs of kokoroko and three shots of tequila, balancing it with chicken wings and fried pork, and then dance like he was releasing all the sexual tension into the world. On Fridays he would meet with the boys after work for rounds of kebab and shots and laughter and conversations on work, life, fantasy football, how ridiculous the men-are-trash movement was, and how they couldn't believe that the women in their lives were proudly tweeting about it as though they didn't have good men like them in their lives. By the end of both nights everybody had heard about Coleen so much we might as well have been dating her too. We also knew all this abstinence talk was temporary.

Every day at noon, Takyi would pass by Coleen's office, where she worked for a regional breakfast-on-wheels startup as an accountant. They'd have lunch together in his company car, and she would kiss him goodbye. But no tongue, though, in case they were further tempted.

After three months Takyi was sexually frustrated, and although he had promised God and Coleen that he would abstain, it was getting harder every day. In hindsight he might have been too hasty promising such a big thing to God too; he should've stuck to just Coleen. And so it wasn't very hard flirting back with Abby from Sales, when she called out to him as he climbed up the stairs after lunch.

"Ei, is all that botoss for you? God paaa and giving things to people who don't need them."

"Yes o, all mine. You should see what it can do in bed."

And that's how they almost kissed in the office during lunch break. Abby had been flirting with him for two straight weeks. She'd become overly friendly, overly touchy, overly conversational. And yes, he should've shut it down the very first time it began, but he missed sexual attraction, missed sex, he wasn't even that much into kissing but he missed even that. So when she inched in closer, although he could tell minutes before it almost happened, he didn't stop it. It was only when her face was a breath away that an uneasy feeling prompted him back to his senses.

Takyi thought to himself, Coleen is somewhere convinced she's finally found the sweetest God-fearing abstaining man she'd always asked God for; praying with her, sending Bible verses, finishing Bible plans together, driving to church with her, all the while never demanding or asking for sex. God-sent. So unlike her ex Eugene. And here he was, leading another girl on. He moved away with an awkward smile and later sent Abby a text message apologizing for the mixed signals. A message she left on read.

The sexual frustration did not dissipate into thin air, but it was cushioned by the guilt of almost kissing Abby, and the fear of losing Coleen.

One Monday, after picking Coleen up from work, they were driving home when Coleen remembered a conversation from work about capitalism and neoliberalism.

"Today the guys in my office—Yoofi and Lawrence, you remember them, right? Yoofi is the bearded bald one, and Lawrence is the tall one with a limp."

"Yeah yeah, I remember Yoofi."

"Yeah. So they were arguing in the office about how capitalism and neoliberalism are the only things that can save Ghana."

"Oh, how?"

"Yeah, Yoofi swears by capitalism and neoliberalism. He says Ghana's long-term track record is nothing to build futures on. And if you look at the country, we are still deep in the trenches of relying on the West. Yes, Nkrumah started off on the right foot, but look at where his Communist ideas have gotten us."

"What?"

"His exact words were 'we are toothless dogs in a cruel game of fetch.'"

"And capitalism is the answer? A thing is only of merit of sustenance and continuation when it is incentivized? First of all, you and I know that only works for the rich. Also fuck neoliberalism chale, every generation thinks they have fresh new ideas and all the old ideas are ineffective. Neoliberals are so cocksure in pointing out the problems of inequality, but when it comes to actually ditching their comfort and fixing it they balk. Diaspora folks come back home as neocoloniz-ers, flaunting their bourgeois selves in attempting solutions borrowed from the West with little regard for what exists. Talmbout 'Yah, I really think we can experiment with this, there's so much opportunity here to explore with technology,' and when that doesn't work they either run back or settle to being oppressors themselves—caring only about their elite selves. So I don't think there's a one-size-fits-all solution as it is or that even has all the answers, but capitalism and so-called neoliberalism sure ain't it."

I think that mini rant must have been the moment that Coleen actually fell for our man. It was as if this discussion was the moment my nigga cupid finally showed up and *piw piw piw* started staking spikes with equal portions of love that Takyi felt into Coleen's chest. It was also the night Coleen got carried away because when Takyi kissed her when dropping her off at home, she felt so soft and yielding that she dipped her tongue into the lap of his welcoming mouth, and when he slipped his fingers underneath her A-line office skirt, she forgot herself. And because she didn't stop it, he took this as the sign to go further, parted her panties to the side, and slid two fingers (the middle and ring finger) up. It lasted for just ten seconds but an upset Coleen came to herself and tumbled out of the car, going to bed without saying good night.

Takyi apologized to Coleen's back, sat in his car for another ten minutes, and drove away with a hard-on.

The timing of the discussion on capitalism and neoliberalism might've been what saved Takyi; had it been any later than that, he might've never heard from Coleen, but because Coleen had confirmed for herself that she was dating an intelligent young man, and even though she was upset, she didn't end the relationship.

One Saturday he and Coleen were stuck in traffic, after attending the youth treasurer's wedding. It was a very beautiful wedding. Coleen was mesmerized by the silver frills interlaced with crystal beading in the bride's dress, and completely jealous of Baaba's (the bride) second outfit for the reception—a nude soft sheer dress that she thought would look absolutely gorgeous on her. She was impressed with her six-member bridal train and their individual dress styles and wouldn't stop talking about it. Takyi himself enjoyed the ceremony tremendously, although so many things about the wedding now had him thinking. He was a little surprised at how the treasurer, Koku, could afford this kind of wedding with three hundred guests in attendance. There's no way he did that on a banker's salary. Or was there? Do banks pay that well? How long had he been saving? Or did his bride chip in? Or their families supported? Or did he take a loan? Surely he can't be that stupid? And Koku had rented a one-bedroom apartment just months ago. Thank God for his parents' house. Thank God his siblings moved out, because more space for him for when he gets married too. Rent plus this costly wedding? That wedding must have cost at least 50,000 cedis. That is just way too much money. Besides, he didn't want a glamorous wedding, he wanted something crafted just for him—not too simple, not too extravagant; right in the middle. And even if he had that kind of money to spare he would rather invest it in a business. He's been wanting to start—

"So where will we stay when we get married?" Coleen asks.

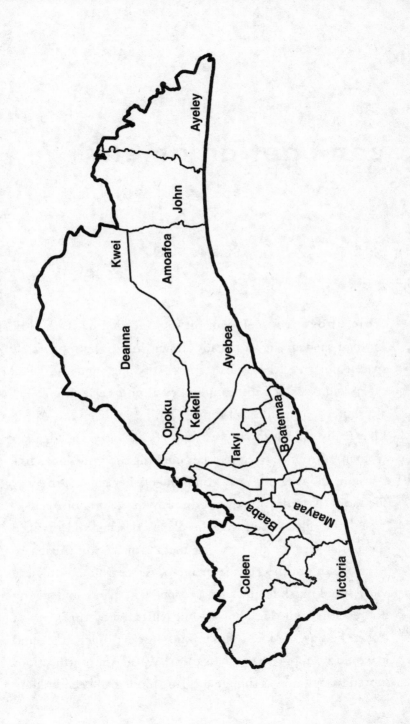

can i get an amen?!

ACCRA, 2021

From above, the colors of the city blended in as if a little kid had shaded out an already drawn map. The moderately spaced-out tree, the asphalt stretch of lines, and the pastel green and brick-red rooftops looked almost harmonious. For a minute, John could feel himself falling in love with Accra. Like really falling for it, you know? The way you drink a woman in from afar without her noticing, how she looks like a vision, the way her sway compliments her curves, the way she looks like a dream covered in brown: the city of Accra.

As the pilot announced the plane's descent and thanked the passengers for flying with them from Addis Ababa to Accra, John breathed in the image of Accra from a bird's-eye view—looking like the city unzipped its pants and gently poured itself out. He allowed himself to enjoy this view of Accra, because he knew the minute his feet touched ground it would be more chaos than calm. WhatsApp notifications started trooping in as though airplane mode had been holding them captive. Ayeley's "you better not be too tired for today, ma guy" flashed on the screen for a second before being pushed down by a flurry of other messages, and it made him smile. He was tired and sleepy, but he wasn't missing this day party for anything.

Two years ago, Baaba had called him at midnight in a terrible state: she'd swallowed eight of her sister's pain pills and pushed them down with a bottle of shocker (an abominable mix of orange juice, vodka, and marijuana). How they managed to get through that night alone was a miracle, but the hard part was after. She was irritable and mean and too quiet and too loud and too spaced out, not sleeping well, not enough energy to get through one thing, not enough joy to push a body through one day. Therapy made things worse. The first therapist she went to tried to use the name of Jesus like it was a brightly colored plaster, the second therapist generalized sexual abuse as a way to soften the hurt, told her that if it helped, most women experienced it, as if sexual assault were a lollipop every woman had to lick before they could become adults. By the time a fitting therapist had been found Baaba had overdressed her vulnerability and taught her pain how to use its inside voice. She looked okay, talked okay, seemed to be doing okay, and had even started seeing some guy she had met in a waakye queue. But John just knew something was broken. She wasn't the same Baaba. It took a lot of emotional bargaining to get her to see Dr. S. but it had been worth it. She was less closed off, less jumpy, her life not dictated by anxiety. And so after eight months of seeing

Dr. S., when Baaba asked if he would go with her to a mental health awareness run, he happily wore the too-tight shirt she got for him and tagged along. That was how he met Ayeley. She was wearing a white T-shirt with a face that wasn't hers on the front of it. With the inscription "Victoria Otu 1990–2018, forever loved." She had a blue marker in her right hand and was trying to write on the back of the T-shirt by gathering the folds to her side. After watching her struggle with it for a few minutes John asked if he could help.

"Thank you so much. My friend Coleen was supposed to be here by now, but she's stuck in traffic so I had to try before it started."

Weeks later he would meet Coleen and Ayeley's fiancé, Ekow, and find out all three were youth members of Ayeley's father's church. They had a Bible study slash book club slash I-only-have-energy-for-drinks-and-gossip hangout once or twice a month. Their monthly meetings were a cozy cherry-red bubble, a sprawling of tired and eager bodies, where you could feel the slab of your arms sticking to the back of someone's shirt, and Coke was water, and tequila was communion for both bad and good days, and voices called dibs on whose turn it was to leave the room to go use the washroom.

And it was there that John would find himself falling for Coleen. It was a slow build. It wasn't deliberate or followed through or even wanted. Because although she rarely talked about her husband, she was taken, and he had no business wanting another man's wife. He was tired of wanting women who were in committed relationships. But desire for her stank on him like the unmistakable scent of a bad fart. You could tell in how his voice got softer when talking to her. How he let her rest her body on him like it was the sole function of his side. The way he slouched through the evening when she didn't show up because Takyi had taken her on a date. How he lit up for her——an exaggerated affection. Everybody with eyes could tell he had fallen for her. So badly that if his mum saw how whipped he was in front of Coleen she would sing-cry Presbyterian songs with her hands pointed towards the sky and double her Sunday offering. John knew it, Coleen knew it, and Ayeley knew it too, because when a new girl joined church she invited her to their monthly ritual in hopes that she would become the new object of John's affection. But it wasn't until two meetings in that they found out the new girl, Amoafoa, was married with an eleven-month-old baby.

For Amoafoa, meeting Ayeley saved her from a dark place she didn't even know she had fallen into. Everything about Ayeley reminded her of Deanna, how articulate her words sounded when she was fixated on something, the way she was committed to talking about cooking dinner like it was some shit that mattered, her loud contagious laughter, how defensive she was of her friends. All of it reminded her of Deanna, and she wasn't sure if that made her happy or want to cry. She missed Deanna terribly, and she knew she could reach out to her or send her another awkward message. But silence had done a good job of severing their bond so that any little effort felt too raw. Finding this new group of people gave her something to look forward to, and even if the end of her year looked dull, at least there was this day party to put a shine to it.

Since the baby, Opoku had grown a beard and looked even more handsome. She felt consumed by her love for him more than his love for her. It wasn't that he demonstrated it less, or that he became any different from who he was when they were dating. It was that the persistent feeling of not being loved well carried itself forward into their marriage. He appeared willing to love her in the way that she desired, but it remained just that—an appearance. She had banked her hopes on marriage being the permission slip to go all out; the loud hurray before you cut the cake and push a tasty slice down your throat. Instead it was the same weak amen; scant details, guardedness, a fuck here and there as he liked, to be guided and helped with care when he needed it, to be given love in measured doses. She expected her heart to have been dulled by this but all it did was yearn for him, and treat the slightest gesture as evidence for continued hope.

And she wished Deanna was still here to mull things over with her, smack some sense into her or sit with her through the tears, but their friendship had sunk too deep to rescue. It had begun with lots of silences. Short explanations. No explanations. Reemerging of closeness. Short emails. No emails. Graceful excuses but still no emails or messages. Then a distancing. She remembered how she had wanted to just show up on her doorstep and hug and cry until they were back to being best friends. She told herself that maybe it was just life or time or circumstances or the both of you picking cues from each other or a mixture of everything. And how wrong she had been.

How wounding friendship can be. You never know there's a bandwidth regulating a relationship until it runs out of steam. You draw further and further apart. You know fully well how much you love each other, yet you cannot convert your feelings into a reasoning tangible enough to comfort you. Until it is too awkward to talk every day, or every seven days—and attempts at closeness feel like an imitation of the real thing, and then it becomes too painful to be awkward. And suddenly, someone you once called best friend, who you were once so close to that they knew how one bad-luck panty burned a hole in the crack of your ass on Thursday—suddenly, you're no longer friends with this someone. You just move from being really good friends to being nothing. There's no breakup text, no bad argument defining the beginning of your ruin. Just a dull ache of unsolvable nothingness.

• • •

In December, Accra looks like a strange form of street theater: sweaty men with toned muscles asking girls to smile for smiling's sake, short women in even shorter skirts daring you to say just one word, pudgy market women with singing mouths, skinny girls with heavy pans and airy pockets, cars breathing on each other's neck, and everybody else caught up in the capitalist gaudiness of stepping outside your house. The number of events that happen inside the city from December

26 to 31 can fill up one quarter of the year: day parties for those who want to preserve nighttime for themselves or for other things, a million and one drinking events, all-white dress-code shows, a thousand weddings, a concert for you, a concert for me, a concert for everybody, church for breakfast, brunch, lunch, dinner, and nighttime snacks, everybody and their mother throwing house parties. It was almost as if a thirst had been festering all throughout the year, waiting to be squeezed out in the last days.

The DUSK party had been advertised since the beginning of December. It was for those who wanted to meet old friends, grind on new bodies, and drink themselves tipsy. But for Boatemaa, Ayebea, and Kekeli, their sole mission was to dance the night away.

The inside of the club resembled stained glass. The lights were halfway dim and halfway bright, tones of red and blue clashing into each other. Being in there felt like you had been pushed slightly and it was an unending game of trying to regain your balance. For someone who planned what she would eat a week ahead, Boatemaa was surprised to have found a friend in Ayebea. She was loud and bossy and a little too risky and took way too much pleasure in being mean to men. But she was also protective and fun and loved *Family Guy* as much as she did. When she took this new job at a petroleum company as a project manager, it had been something to occupy her for a year at least, before she started her masters, but here she was, two years later, actually happy with a 9-to-5 and with two work best friends she did almost everything with.

It didn't take Ayebea less than five minutes to ditch them. It was inevitable; men flocked to her like she was literal shit, and the girls had gotten used to it. Boatemaa downed her drink and pulled Kekeli to the dance floor.

The music was not memorable, but it was movable. Efya's "Nothing" started to play. Once the refrain began, it spread through the girls' bodies; it passed through Kekeli's arms and enfolded itself in the swell of her hips, and then it let itself loose in her legs. It rocked Boatemaa's soft bosom into a playful wiggle, sent its infectious rhythm along the insides of her belly, dislodging the tension in her waist into an eager dance. They laughed for no reason, singing along to *baby, there's nothing that I wouldn't do for you, for you, for you, for you.*

As they danced Kekeli felt joy. She couldn't remember the last time she had been this happy. There was a time when sadness swelled in her like the high note of a Mariah Carey song; so poisoned by her unhappiness that she could not remember a time when she had known joy or imagined it in the future. She felt her phone vibrate and she pulled it from her jeans pocket. It was her father letting her know that he would be up late, just in case she preferred him as her chauffeur for the night instead of a taxi. If her heart could burst out of her chest from the weight of her contentedness, it would at this very moment. Who ever thought that she would one day call her father friend? That there was a place for infinite tenderness in being someone's daughter. She had a persistently depressed mood to thank for her new relationship with her father. She didn't wish to ever go back to that period of her life after the abortion, but she could be thankful that her not wanting to live caused her father to be intentional about loving his daughter like she needed to be loved. All this time, she had come to understand being her parents' child as a thing that didn't allow her to be her own person, living up to a template laid out for her and leaving little space for her to cast her own mold. But somehow, in the midst of despair churning deep in her gut, her father had carved space for her to breathe. Soon they made a ritual out of walking down the dusty streets of Taifa Burkina, talking about small and unimportant things, big and scary things. Going on drives (to the annoyance of her mother), catching up on life, and discovering new music despite calling each other's taste questionable. And here too, she learned to see her father as a person, and not just an adult male belonging to the role of fatherhood. She learned to unravel him from a marble statue of rules and high standards to a soft malleable shape of affection.

Wizkid's voice sent a jolt of overexcitement into Boatemaa and she moved a little too quickly, sharply bumping into someone. She turned to apologize and Opoku's face stared back at her. For the briefest of seconds, time froze: she had forgotten how long it was since she last saw or thought of him. She had stopped counting the days after she went past 287. Last she had heard, he had gotten married in Amoafoa's mother's backyard, the bride in a stunning green kente dress and French plaits. And here he was dancing with a girl who was not Amoafoa. It surprised her how much she felt at peace, how promptly she felt tickled. It surprised her that there used to be a time when she had felt bound by her emotions for this man, unable to see a future beyond their togetherness, so much that it had maimed her individual functionality when that future was threatened. And here she was, she unfettered and him forgotten.

An apology made its way out of her mouth, but the mixture of surprise and awkwardness on his face greatly tickled her. She tried to stop it, she really did, but a grand bubbly laughter rose from her throat and spilled out of her mouth like a prosperity sermon.

Acknowledgments

This book exists because I have an agent who respects and values my writing, but most importantly, cares about how it exists in the world. Thank you, Rena.

Immensely grateful for Sara Levin, whose guidance and thoughtfulness has shaped my storytelling for the better.

I wish to particularly thank Jennifer Baker, whom I began editing with. Although I didn't finish the editing process with Jen, her incredible eye for detail and nuanced suggestions did not leave me—or this book. I am grateful to Daniella Wexler and Ghjulia Romiti at Amistad for their thoughtful suggestions and attentiveness too.

Thank you to Sharanya, Ife, and Pemi, for being another pair of (incredibly gifted) eyes for these stories.

And finally, thank you to the editors of *Astra Magazine* and *MQR Mixtape*, where "Drip" and "Hand-Me-Down" first appeared.